Ajivika's Laughter

Ajivika's Laughter

Surendra Mohanty

Translated from Odia by
Sambit Panigrahi

BLACK EAGLE BOOKS
2021

BLACK EAGLE BOOKS

USA address:
7464 Wisdom Lane
Dublin, OH 43016

India address:
E/312, Trident Galaxy, Kalinga Nagar,
Bhubaneswar-751003, Odisha, India

E-mail: info@blackeaglebooks.org
Website: www.blackeaglebooks.org

First International Edition Published by
BLACK EAGLE BOOKS, 2020

AJIVIKA'S LAUGHTER
by **Surendra Mohanty**
Translated by **Sambit Panigrahi**

Original Copyright © With the family members of Surendra Mohanty
Translation Copyright © **Sambit Panigrahi**

Cover & Interior Design: Ezy's Publication

ISBN- 978-1-64560-197-5 (Paperback)
Library of Congress Control Number: 2021942601

Printed in the United States of America

Translator's Note

Surendra Mohanty, an eminent Odia writer and politician, was born on 21 June 1922 and died on 21 December 1990. A writer of unique creative acumen, Mohanty wrote many fictional and non-fictional works that continue to remain his significant contribution to the immense literary reservoir of Odia language. Apart from being a writer of great eminence, Mohanty also held many important literary and political positions in the state. He was the president of Odisha Sahitya Academy from 1981 to 1987 and was also the first editor, and later chief editor for the newspaper *The Sambad*. He was a writer of short stories, novels, travelogues, criticism and biographies; he wrote around 50 books belonging to different genres. Some of his well-known novels are *Nilasaila* (*The Blue Mountain*) and *Andha Diganta* (*The Dark Horizon*) whereas some of his famous short stories include stories like "Mahanirvana" ("The Salvation"), "Yadubansa" ("The Yadu Dynasty"), "Mahanagarira Ratri? ("Night in the City"), "Rajadhani" ("The Capital City"), "Krushnachuda" ("The Gulmohar") and "Ruti O Chandra" ("Bread and Moon").

Apart from being a litterateur, he was also a politician and a member of parliament many times from 1957 onwards.

Translating Surendra Mohanty is an experience in itself. It's widely acknowledged by literary critics that by producing an enormous body of literary works that include novels and short stories and travel writings, Surendra Mohanty has been able to establish himself as one of the finest writers in Odia language. The most interesting feature about his novels and short stories is that they are not confined to any particular theme or area; rather, they range across a wide variety of subject matters including history, mythology, his contemporary society, the individual etc. The wide spectrum of themes, areas and concerns that he encompasses in his novels and stories provide him wide acceptability as a writer amongst the audience. Mohanty seems to have developed a particular interest in Buddhism and its history for which he has penned some of his stories like "Pita Putra" ("Father and Son") and "Mahanirvana" ("The Salvation") and novels like *Ajivikara Attahasya* (Ajivika's Laughter). In my estimation, some of Mohanty's finest writings are in fact his novels and stories based on Buddhism and its history.

As mentioned by me, Mohanty takes particular interest in history and mythology whose biggest testimony is his novel *Ajivikara Attahashya* (translated by me as *Ajivika's Laughter*)— which is a historical novel based on Buddhism's tremendous moral and ethical deterioration after Lord Buddha's 'parinirvana[1].' Though Mohanty in his "Preface" to this book categorically denies an absolute allegiance to History and its verifiable facts, still one can get a sufficiently clear picture of Buddhism's declining moral and ethical status after its prophet's death and it becoming a potent tool in the hands of Monarch Ashoka to maintain his vast and expansive kingdom's territorial sovereignty. We come to know how Buddhism gradually lost its spiritual appeal and progressively became a political tool in the hands of monarch Ashoka who craftily manipulated the religion to transform his own image of a destroyer 'Kalashoka/Chandashoka' to that of an extremely religious 'Dharmashoka.' When the whole world celebrates such an unbelievable transformation of monarch Ashoka after the Kalinga War[2] and hails this transformed king as a preserver and propagator of

---

[1] The ultimate attainment of salvation.
[2] A fierce war that was fought in 262 BC between kingdoms of Magadha and Kalinga where the latter was beaten and thoroughly decimated by the orders of the Magadha king Ashoka.

humanitarian values, this novel poses a serious question to such claims and depicts the monarch as an unchanged and monstrous character who cunningly used his conversion to Buddhism as a pretext to his so-called transformation. According to Mohanty, Ashoka was never a changed man and continued to remain equally bloodthirsty and exploitative as he was before the *Kalinga War*, though he made a few concerted efforts to project a different image of his to the world by using his conversation to Buddhism as a pretext.

Moreover, the novel also traces the trajectories through which Buddhism progressively underwent a decline so far as its moral and ethical standings were concerned in a scenario where there were other evolving strands of thought and philosophy that questioned and, in a way, dismantled the very core and foundation of the Buddhist philosophy. The Ajivika community was one such community that was radically opposed to the latter's advocacy of self-abnegation as the only means towards the attainment of salvation. Instead, they provided a thoroughly destiny-oriented philosophy of life and advocated the notion that one need not denounce his body for achieving salvation and there is no moral and ethical wrong committed through the unhindered indulgence in bodily pleasures as everything is governed by the omnipotent destiny. Their destiny-oriented philosophy attracted many Buddhist disciples towards them and they happily denounced Buddhism to become a part of the Ajivika community. This conflict between the Ajivikas and the Buddhists is brilliantly depicted by Mohanty through the characters of the disciples, Upananda and Kshema who renounced Buddhism to accept a constraint-free and licentious way of life as a pathway towards the attainment of salvation—a way that was categorically proposed and advocated by the Ajivika community. In a way, this novel interrogates Buddhism's ability to remain a thoroughly sanctified and unadulterated religion after the demise of its prophet Buddha.

Apart from the above-mentioned thematic delineations and ventures, the novel also casts an investigative glance at the illustrious historical figure, monarch Ashoka of the great Mauryan empire. Taking a radically different course and direction that might seem preposterously maverick to many, the novel intends to puncture and de-sanctify the celebratory, religious image that History has benevolently attributed to monarch Ashoka. The novel challenges the notion that monarch Ashoka was a thoroughly transformed man after the infamous *Kalinga War* and delineates that the monarch continued to remain equally savage, heinous and bloodthirsty even after the devastations of the war. In this respect, the novel claims to remain a unique endeavour on the author's part to challenge History's monopoly over truth and presents alternative versions of History that do exist yet go unrecognized.

After providing a brief introduction to some of the important thematic concerns of Mohanty in the mentioned novel, I must now share with the audience some of my own experiences of translating Mohanty from Odia to English. It is famously said by eminent American poet Robert Frost that "Poetry is what is lost in translation"—a statement that is a clear indicator of how much difficult it is for the translator to carry the whole essence of the original text into the translated text. Each language is intrinsically embedded with certain cultural values and nuances specific to its own and which are perhaps untranslatable. Certain colloquial expressions, which Mohanty abundantly uses in his writing, are its best example. As a translator of Mohanty's novels and short stories, I have tried my level best to negotiate between two languages and two cultures that are, without even an iota of doubt, diametrically opposite to each other. It must be understood nevertheless that absolute faithfulness to the original text and the original language is an absolute impossibility.

Mohanty, in spite of his greatness and stature as a creative writer in Odia, can at times be accused of unwarranted verbosity though I do understand that a creative writer's creative process has limitless dimensions. Translating wordy sentences and expressions may look a bit challenging, but it is also a pleasurable experience to translate the clumsiness of certain colloquial, ornate and verbose expressions in the original language, i.e. Odia and re-present them in a simplified form in the target language, that is English.

At the end, I would like to thank my family members including my parents and my wife and friends who stood by me all through my effort. And at last my prayer to Lord Jagannath.

Sambit Panigrahi

Author's Preface

In Third Century BC, and during the reign of the Mauryan dynasty's monarch Ashoka, also infamously known as Kalashoka or Chandashoka, a huge Buddhist conference was organized in Baisali where Buddhism was divided into two factions: Hinajana and Mahajana. This historical novel is written on the mentioned backdrop. But it must be clarified at the outset that in this novel, History is no more than a mere skeletal structure, an overarching fabric. Though this novel endeavours to present an overall picture of the third Century BC, most characters in this book are fictional ones except a few real historical characters like monarch Ashoka, Acharya Upali, Acharya Rebata and Acharya Kashyapa etc. whose existence during the mentioned era is, of course, historically verifiable. But the possibility of many other imaginary characters introduced in the novel existing in reality during the mentioned period of time cannot be entirely discounted either. These are some representational figures of the era discussed in the novel and some such characters are bound to find place in a work of this kind that intends to recreate that bygone, antediluvian era before the readers with all earnestness, or at least a semblance of that era. Without the instauration of these characters and figures, the book would seemingly lose its attractive fictionality and would turn out to be a mere, bland and desiccated historical document, not a historical novel.

Gautama Buddha's propagated religion of Buddhism was a religious institution run by stringent rules, principles and regulations where self-abnegation was the primary and inviolable dictum. His indoctrinations were based on the fundamental argument that if one can attain salvation by following his primitive, bestial instincts, then what is the need for prolonged religious perseverance? Instinct leads one towards the murky path of bestiality, but never leads him to the holy and sanctified realm of divinity which, as per Buddha's preachings, could be achieved only through self-abnegation. Gautama Buddha believed that realization of divinity is the cardinal principle and the fundamental ethical foundation of every religion and in this realization, is embedded a human being's unrelenting progression towards salvation.

In this scenario, Lord Buddha's advocation of his Ten Commandments for his male and female disciples, was directed at the inculcation of a sense of discipline inside the pious and ensconced premises of this religious community. After his 'parinirvana,' nevertheless, the religion had been progressively riven by innumerable internal ideological conflicts and undercurrents for which it had started continually losing its erstwhile impact and relevance. As a counteractive measure to curb this deteriorative scenario, the first Buddhist council was organized in Rajagruha under the royal patronage of the then Magadha king Ajatasatru, almost immediately after Lord Buddha's 'parinirvana.' In this conference was witnessed a restructuration of the religion's organizational fabric through the introduction of more stringency and austerity in terms of the observation of its rules, regulations and principles with the anticipation that the religion would remain permanently safeguarded from the rancorous encroachment of the vices like immorality, adultery and licentiousness. The self-righteous stewards of the community were now contentedly assured that their religion shall thrive to exist at least for ten thousand years; but disillusionment set in when they witnessed rampant and indiscriminate violations of their formulated principles, particularly by the large contingents of young and deviant disciples that had entered into the religion, of late.

These repeated violations, either small or big in

magnitude, generated humongous ideological conflicts amongst the monks of the institution in a scenario where the older ones strictly observed the rules while the newer ones were hell-bent on their gross and persistent violation and infringement. Due to such bizarre and obnoxious developments, the religion was moving towards the dark Hell of absolute blasphemy and thoroughgoing annihilation and to rescue it from utmost degradation, the second Buddhist council was organized in Baisali, under the aegis of the then ruling monarch Ashoka of the illustrious Mauryan empire. A major portion of this novel is dedicated towards the delineation of the mentioned conflict in greater details.

I shall specifically draw the readers' attention on the numerous misconceptions nurtured in history about the Mauryan monarch Ashoka. According to the Singhalese Buddhist tradition, the second Buddhist conference occurred during the reign of a monarch called 'Kalashoka' whereas the North Indian Buddhist tradition confirms 'Kalashoka' and 'Chandashoka' to be one and the same person. These epithets are of course succinctly emblematic of the inherently cruel and savage bestiality exuded by this bloodthirsty monarch whose anecdotes of savagery and bestiality go unparalleled in the prolonged history of humankind. The historians are fully cognizant of the ugly historical truth that before getting formally coroneted as the Mauryan Empire's monarch in 273 BC, Ashoka had mercilessly slaughtered his ninety-nine brothers and his other kith and kin to occupy the throne. But due to the political turmoil generated in Pataliputra because of this familial infighting, his coronation was delayed by four years from the actual day of his occupancy of the throne. In this novel, I have accepted 'Kalashoka,' 'Chandashoka' and monarch Ashoka as the same person during whose reign of unprecedented pogrom and bloodbath, was held the second largest Buddhist convention in Magadha's capital city of Baisali.

Thirteen years after his unlawful coronation, Ashoka had initiated a ruthless pogrom of the innocent Kalingas in the name of his quintessential penchant for territorial expansion. Maddened by the desire of being the undisputed monarch of the whole of Aryabarta[3], Ashoka initiated war against the hitherto unconquered feudal state of Kalinga—an ugly, savage and blasphemous truth that has been encrypted by himself on the rock edicts in Dhauli. In the Kalinga history, nevertheless, one does not find any mention of any Kalinga King's name during Ashoka's humongous and annihilative invasion. As per Ashoka's own delineations in the mentioned inscriptions regarding the devastations in the war, one lakh Kalingas were slaughtered; one lakh and half were taken prisoners to Pataliputra and the same numbers of people were injured. The historians might contentedly depict this savage and ruthless slaughterer as a subsequently transformed man; but this is nothing but a blatant and ostentatious lie. In my estimation, another savage, ruthless and power-craving monarch in Indian history that could match Ashoka's bestiality could only be none other than the heinous and bloodthirsty Mogul monarch Aurangzeb.

But it's a matter of utter shame and disgust that we the Kalingas have also accepted 'Chandashoka' as a subsequently transformed 'Dharmashoka' despite the undeniable truth that this cruel and vicious monarch had slaughtered lakhs of our innocent ancestors without mercy. How could they forget that this savage and homicidal monarch had turned the holy waters of River Daya into a stinking, malodorous pool of blood? But instead, we have started eulogizing him as a transformed, venerable, Buddhist monk. We have shamelessly become like the sheep-herds that sacrifice themselves for the host's betterment and in this scenario, I urge the Kalinga historians not to unjustly eulogize this 'Chandashoka' turned 'Dharmashoka' anymore for in my honest estimation, he is nothing more than a savage and ruthless mass-murderer.

---

[3]   Refers to the undivided Indian subcontinent dominated by the Aryan community during the mentioned period of time.

As a firm evidence of the falsity of Ashoka's so called innate, spiritual transformation, one finds, in his inscriptions, hardly any mention of Gautama Buddha or Buddhism for that matter whereas they are mostly filled with eulogies of Ashoka himself. But on the other hand, in the 'Elephant Cave' inscriptions of great Kalinga monarch Kharabela, one can find multiple eulogies encrypted on both the Buddhists and the Jainists, as insignias of the monarch's selfless adoration of the different religions existing during his time. But of course, one could still find a few Buddhist sermons encrypted on some of Ashoka's inscriptions too; but they are purposely scanty and they eulogize Ashoka much more than they eulogize the Buddhist monks.

It's also grossly undeniable that many monarchs in History have used religion as a tool to control their subjects and Ashoka is no exception. Quite irrefutably, he used Buddhism as a potent tool to safeguard the territorial integrity of his bloodily constructed empire for the baffled public, sentimentally swayed by the religion's overarching influence, never turned unruly and rebellious against the monarch. But the fact remains that a heinous and cruel   monarch like Ashoka could never have been a Buddhist monk, neither a true Buddhist monk could ever have been a monarch like him. To expose this rancorous tyrant's real, dark and sinister face was one of my prime objectives while venturing into writing this novel. I hope that after reading this work, the audience shall be able to recognize the true, ugly face of the mass-murderer Ashoka.

Here I must provide some preliminary information on the Ajivika community that finds a mention in my novel. Of course, this novel does not bear any direct connection to the community as such; but an Ajivika monk has been an important and defining character in this novel, particularly at the initial and the concluding portions of the book. Therefore, I must provide, at this juncture, some fundamental grounding about the weird, eclectic and heretical life and philosophy of the Ajivika community.

During the end of the Upanishadic era and in between the tenth and forth/fifth century BCs (the historical period when the Buddhist and the Jainist religious movements were gaining momentum), the entire Aryan community was divided into multiple factions on the basis of different religious orientations and belief-systems. There were primarily two reasons behind it. One of them was that Vedic Brahmanism, being too much orthodox, abstruse and ritualistic in nature, was beyond the common people's easy comprehension of the religion's dictums and principles. Moreover, the polytheist nature of the Aryan religious practices was entirely baffling and misleading for the common populace due to which their spiritual needs remained thoroughly unattended. In addition, the system of casteism introduced by the Brahmins created an intensely classified society and thus initiated an outrageous saga of exploitation and torture on the downtrodden. So, a large section of this downtrodden class was constantly on the lookout for new religious leaders who would cater to their spiritual requirements, which in fact were now fulfilled with the emergence of a new group of non-Vedic and non-Brahminical leaders. It must be mentioned emphatically that none amongst Prophet Mahabir Jain of Jainism, Prophet Gautama Buddha of Buddhism, Prophet Makhali Gosala of the Ajivika community and Prophet Charbak of the Charbak community belonged to the Vedic and the Brahminical tradition. In the combined effects of these prophets, the Vedic religion was almost wiped out from North India.

Secondly, during these times the common populace of the whole Aryan landscape was always exposed to warfare, plunder and pogrom from both inside and outside. From inside, they were subject to persistent attacks and atrocities by the territorially expansive kingdoms like Magadha and Koshala etc. whereas from outside, their existence was perennially threatened by the external invaders like the Greeks, the Huns, the Kuchis and the Kushans. Tortured, tormented and devastated by these recurrent attacks, atrocities and humiliations, the common people needed peace and solace which these newly emerging religious groups intended to provide them.

The Ajivika community was one amongst these different, emerging religious communities. A contemporary of Lord Buddha, Makhali Gosala is universally accepted to be this community's indubitable prophet. It is said that during his sojourn towards the attainment of 'nirvana,' the Lord had spent some time with Makhali Gosala's Ajivika community; but their unrestrained, bohemian and renegade lifestyle could not bind him for long. He developed serious differences of opinion with the Ajivikas, at an ideological level, abandoned them and left alone on his way towards his preordained salvation-seeking destination. So, the Ajivikas always hated the Buddha and never hesitated to indulge in his character-assassination, if they got the slightest opportunity.

They ran a fabricated story that the Buddha, while living in Koshala's 'Benubana Vihara,' had impregnated a Brahmin widow named Kinka; the ill-intentioned maneuvers of the Ajivikas are elaborately mentioned in the holy Buddhist scriptures. One of Lord Buddha's cousins Devadutta was closely associated with the Ajivika community and was a diehard follower of their utterly libertine culture and unrestricted and unprincipled way of life. The Buddhist scriptures also mention how he instigated king Ajatasatru for patricide and also tried, once upon a time, to eliminate Gautama Buddha by dint of an evil design.

Ajivikas were staunch believers in destiny and never believed in the dialectics of good/bad, religious/non-religious etc., neither were they interested, in any way, to make unwarranted moral value judgments about people and things. According to one of the gurus of the community Ajita-Kesha-Kambali, there is no piety in getting up early, taking bath and worshipping gods, neither is there any sin in slaughtering hundreds of animals every morning. Whatever is predestined shall happen. It may be mentioned at this juncture that the same philosophy was prevalent in the ancient Sumerian and Greek cultures of those times and one can witness clear instances of such thoughts and practices in Homer's illustrious epic *The Iliad*. From these destiny-believing traits of the Sumerians, emerged Astrology as a branch of knowledge. But of course, it won't be appropriate to ascertain that this branch of knowledge flowed into the Indian subcontinent from the Sumerians only. The destiny-believing trait has always been a global phenomenon and it was inherently ingrained in the philosophical and discursive practices in the Indian subcontinent just the way it was present in the Greek and the Sumerian civilizations. Of course, the Ajivika community was its major proponent in the Indian subcontinent.

The six prophets of the Ajivika community were:

1-Purana Kashyapa

2-Makhhali Gosala

3-Ajita Keshakambali

4-Pakuddha Kachhayana

5-Sanjaya Belathiputta

6-Nigantha Nathaputta

Due to their expertise in fortune-telling, they were extremely popular amongst the common masses, and even amongst the people of royalty. For this reason, many kings including Ajatasatru had become their disciples. Due to the enormous influence of the Ajivika community on the ancient Indian culture and philosophy, their destiny-oriented philosophy has been recurrently mentioned in many cantos of *The Geeta*. In these cantos, the human destiny is attributed preponderance over the questions of good and evil deeds in a human being's life. Of course, to enter into these prolonged and complicated details shall amount to be an enormously strenuous exercise and would be an unnecessary digression at this point in time.

As a principle, Ajivikas were perennially opposed to Gautama Buddha's archetypal indoctrinations of renouncement and self-abnegation. They argued that the foundational principles of Buddhism were feeble and unsustainable due to their hardnosed suppression of the basic human instinct and perhaps because of which it crumbled to different segments and factions within a century of its birth. The Ajivikas had always been mockers of Buddhism.

This novel was written by me in 1986. I must owe my gratitude to my son Puspamitra who had taken immense pains to pen the novel from my dictation and to prepare the final manuscript for publication. But without his contribution, this novel could not have been published. I must also thank the editor of Saptarshi Press Sri Baikunthanatha Acharya for the correction of proof that he performed with tremendous fortitude and concentration. Finally, I must thank the publisher *Cuttack Students' Store* who took initiative to publish the novel as quickly as possible. Let Lord Buddha bless everybody who has contributed to this novel in some way or other.

Surendra Mohanty

Shibani, Cuttack-8
September 23, 1987

C O N T E N T S

Chapter I

On the bank of River Sadanira, was situated the city of Baisali of the Lichhavis[4].

Lord Gautama Buddha himself had sermonized to them about penance and self-abnegation here in Baisali and had turned its abject and sleazy atmosphere into a holy and sanctified one. Slowly the city was converted into an illustrious Buddhist centre where its disciples chanted sermons collectively, every morning and every evening; their chantings infused into its unsavoury and mundane atmosphere an unmatchable spiritual candour and sanctitude. With the progress of time, the city's holy and deified environment attracted into its midst large contingents of disciples and gurus from every nook and corner of the kingdom of Magadha and with their relentless influx and advent, Baisali rose to its heydays of sanctimony and religiosity.

Lord Buddha's divine touch was ingrained in the city's heart and soul—apotheosized and extolled by his holy blessings that percolated through the air with the soothing fragrance of divinity. He had benevolently accepted the city-courtesan Amrapalli's hospitality here in this Baisali and had spent some auspicious time here while sermonizing the city-dwellers about the prospects of the attainment of 'nirvana' through the practice of self-abnegation. And coming under his sacred influence, Amrapalli had gleefully adopted Buddhism and subsequently, had transformed herself into Theri[5] Amrapalli.

---

4   An old and ancient clan of the kingdom of Magadha.
5   A term for a female Buddhist monk.

She had converted her luxurious mango orchard into 'Mahabana Vihara'—a renowned and enshrined Buddhist hermitage and had gifted its protracted premises for the growth and proliferation of this sacred religious community. Before his demise, the Lord had delivered his last sermons here and had consecrated its begrimed soil with the holy and deific touch of his divine feet. That is how 'Mahabana Vihara' turned out to be the most illustrious and glorious religious destination not only in Baisali, but perhaps in the entire landscape of the vast, expansive Aryabarta.

Upananda and Kshema were thrown away from 'Mahabana Vihara' through a punishment meted out to them by the rigid and principle-abiding Acharya[6] Kashyapa, one amongst the most nonpareil and sanctimonious stewards of the community. The community had also appropriated his action through a massive and unambiguous referendum. The blasphemous duo was no more welcome in the community's holy and ensconced premises and had become ignominious outcastes after their willful and blatant violation of 'dharma.'

Upananda however was not ready to accept the punishment without interrogating its justifiability and legitimacy. A buoyant and bellicose spirit flared up inside his disgruntled mind and his intractable soul asked repeatedly: "Why this huge retribution? What is our crime? What is truth? Instinct or abnegation?"

He kept pondering over these questions unremittingly and at some point, was convinced that both were true.

Disciples Upananda and Kshema, after being dispelled from 'Mahabana Vihara,' wandered aimlessly through the circuitous depths of the Sal forest with wounded hearts and reproachful minds. They wanted to revolt. Their destination was uncertain and thus, their sojourn was tireless and continuous. They drifted away like two dry leaves along River Sadanira's banks and through the depths of the adjacent Sal

---

6   A prestigious and respectable way of accosting a guru.

forest that stretched before them like an unforeseen enigma, like an insolvable perplexity. Perhaps their ultimate destination was Magadha's Pataligrama. While strolling through the unending and impervious forest, they were lost in their own wild and inexpressible thoughts and they kept gliding aimlessly into the former's endless expanses of mystery and obfuscation. They had no feeling of fear or apprehension or remorse, neither did they harbour any sense of certitude and hopefulness about their future. Theirs was an aimless sojourn in an unknown direction, a liberation from their tainted, sacrilegious past, a mindless progression into an uncertain yet exhilarating future.

They had managed to spend the last night in an Ajivika monk's leaf-cottage. But where would they stay tonight? While contemplating over tonight's stay, they felt in their haggard bodies and fatigued minds the strenuous exhaustion of relentless walking through the forest's interminable, winding paths. It had drained their exhausted bodies off the last residues of their youthful energy and enthusiasm that they had carried all along despite their humiliating ouster from the community. It seemed to them as if the Ajivika monk's rollicking laughter was following them all through like an enigma, a nagging, unanswered question, a stifling interrogation; it had penetrated deep into the dark and vacuous spaces of their minds and had created a massive and stirring upheaval there. The laughter had not yet stopped. That man was a mad Ajivika.

Ajivika was pontificating: "Neither instinct nor abnegation holds eternal significance in a human being's life and existence fraught with the vicissitudes of his unalterable destiny. It is the supreme authority over human life; it is omnipotent, omniscient, omnipresent. There is no grandeur in staunch and steadfast self-abnegation; neither is there any sin or blasphemy committed through its manifest violation. Man is above the futile questions of sin or piety and to enmesh him in these absurd and vain excogitations is nothing but mere stupidity and mindlessness. Man is an inculpable, blameless creature at the mercy of his own destiny."

Yet, Upananda and Kshema were terribly distraught and irritated by the monk's continual and inexorable laughter. They kept guessing that it was intended at them only, and also at their appalling helplessness. However, the monk had told them reassuringly: "Folks! My laughter is directed not towards you, rather towards Lord Buddha who, despite his profound and incomparable erudition, could not comprehend this simple, irrefutable and fundamental truth of human life."

But Upananda and Kshema continued surmising that the monk was trying to fool them around and his laughter was indeed directed at them and at their deplorable plight.

Kshema asked in a tired voice: "How long shall we keep moving, Upananda? Where are we heading, by the way?" She had already asked this question multiple times to him. Upananda could readily trace numerous frowns of restlessness flooding across her fair, rubicund face.

He answered: "I have no idea Kshema. The path of liberation is always atrociously strenuous and painstaking like this, as you see."

Their destination Pataligrama was still a long way.

Upananda and Kshema kept strolling through the forest with an excruciating sense of melancholy and frustration. They kept ruminating that the punishment meted out to them by their dear community was outrageously cruel and unjust and it was thrust upon them with a blatant exhibition of extreme cruelty coupled with utter callousness. They strolled through the forest's marauding decay and dampness; it had dragged them deceptively into its labyrinthine depths and then, had flung them mercilessly onto the glittering sunshine of river Sadanira's banks.

Upananda and Kshema reminded themselves of the 'Repentance Day' in Baisali; here for the first time, they had confronted their own ineluctable reality, and had realized the gravity of their moral turpitude. This realization was terrifying yet enlightening, reprehensible yet self-actualizing; it had toppled their worlds upside down; it had transformed them into different beings, into radically altered and enlightened individuals.

It was the 'Repentance Day' in Baisali's 'Mahabana Vihara.' On this day at every month-end, the disciples voluntarily confessed their sins before a mass gathering of their fellow disciples and gurus and cleansed themselves of their tormenting and vexatious guilts and fallibilities. On a similar occasion, once the Magadha king Ajatasatru had confessed patricide before the Buddha in a 'Repentance Day' and had rid himself of opprobrious blasphemy.

The spring day's golden dusk had adequately faded into the overflowing emptiness of the sprawling and expansive horizon. 'Mahabana Vihara's inmates confessed their sins and repented before Acharya Kashyapa, one after another and went to their respective chambers—happy and contented about getting disburdened, through their confessions, of their lewd sins, moral transgressions and ethical ineptitudes. One amongst the disciples approached the Acharya with a sorrow-laden face, genuflected before him, paid soulful obeisance to him and said: "Forgive me Acharya. Forgive me. I have perpetrated an inexpiable blunder. I have taken meal in my host's house after sunset." His lips were trembling; his eyes were schmaltzy; he was burning in the purgatory fire of repentance. Eating meal in the host's house after sunset was an austerely prohibited practice in the religion and was considered as a profanatory transgression of 'dharma.' Another disciple confessed: "Acharya! I had stealthily concealed salt in my horn-made-pot. I ate salt-mixed food in the host's house." Confessing this, he started sobbing intermittently before the Acharya, and after some time, departed into his chamber with a sullen, despondent and penitential face. This was again a proscribed behavior in Buddhism for mixing salt in food was feared to enhance its deliciousness, sacrilegiously. It would have incited greed in the disciple's mind.

Acharya Kashyapa listened to these little anecdotes of repentance with tremendous fortitude and forbearance, but was thoroughly exhausted at the day's fag end. At the end, he peered into the bluish sky eliciting an expression of compelling desperation on his face, and in his frenzied imagination saw Lord Buddha meditating across its limitless firmament with his quiescent eyes half-closed, and his shimmering right hand lifted into the sky in a posture to bless and liberate tormented humankind. A beatific smile splayed on his face and spread through the pestilential horizon and diffused into the infinite emptiness of the azure sky, like resplendent sunlight diffusing through thickening masses of accumulated fog. Acharya Kashyapa paid obeisance to Buddha with folded hands and pleaded with earnestness: "Save your religion my Lord! Save your religion! These young disciples are unruly; they are deviant; they are unscrupulous; they are irreverent. They don't observe 'dharma' and keep indulging in ignominious worldly acts of impiety and profanation. They will destroy your holy religion, my Lord. They will destroy your holy religion." The momentous concerns on his wearisome face were remarkably evident; the proliferating frowns on his forehead were getting deeper and longer and curvier. The community's progressive degeneration was glaringly manifest and visible; it was unbearable for him to see his beloved religion's rampant and cataclysmic deterioration right in front of his eyes, and not being able to countervail such unabashed and conspicuous decadence, with the impeccable force and vivacity of his religious austerity. He wished he could stop the illimitable influx of these young, perverted and devious disciples into his religion's pious and ensconced territory, and save his religion from ultimate and thoroughgoing desecration. They were eating up its holy and sanctified fabric like ravenous throngs of termites. The Acharya was at his wit's end and didn't know what to do.

But where were these two? These gruesome violators of 'dharma'! Upananda and Kshema! Acharya Kashyapa had heard indiscriminate anecdotes about them and their persistent deviance from the sanctified domains of moral and ethical rectitude. In his honest estimation, they were proven outlaws;

they had turned into prurient beasts. They certainly had no other destination than the 'Abhichi' Hell[7].

Acharya Kashyapa had become thoroughly exhausted after the whole day's fasting. Old age had descended on his bald head, his sunken eyes and his emaciated body like a monotonous and depressing evening. He desperately looked for some rest; but disciples Upananda and Kshema had not yet arrived for repentance. But of course, the inmates who were unwilling to repent never came for the same, neither was it an obligatory compulsion for them that they had to perform mandatorily against their free, independent volition. But Upananda and Kshema's moral transgressions were unpardonable and had crossed all limits of decency, propriety and sanctimony. Their outrageous saga of amorality had spread through the common populace like an ineffaceable hearsay. They had become grisly and grotesque violators of 'dharma' and thus, appalling threats to the religion.

Of course, a few months ago, once disciple Upananda had candidly and wholeheartedly confessed before him on a 'Repentance Day': "O Lord! I am getting irresistibly attracted towards disciple Kshema nowadays. I am no more able to concentrate in my meditation and am getting distracted by her sheer presence in my vicinity, or even by the mere cognition of her presence and 'being.' On the air, float before me Kshema's beautiful face, her attractive pair of lips and her lovely, delicate breasts thereby enticing my reticent and reposeful stoic mind into the filthy quagmire of sin and adultery. When I look at the brimming profusion of voluptuousness on her fleshy body, I lose my deific composure and feel like merging into her like a desperate river flinging itself onto the awaiting sea's infinite nudity. I feel like clinging to her denuded body like a curvaceous creeper coiled, circuitously, around a stolid tree's gigantic trunk. Please forgive me Acharya! I cannot resist my attraction towards her even after being fully cognizant of the fact that such profane

---

[7]   The lowest level of Hell.

and sublunary infatuations are blasphemous, sinful and reprobate. I am falling a hapless prey to this ignoble human fallibility, Acharya; it gnaws my conscious 'self' from inside like an ugly and rapacious monster."

Acharya Kashyapa admonished Upananda: "From now onwards, you will stay away from her proximity like staying away from a poisonous snake. If she appears before you, by dint of an unexpected coincidence, you will close your eyes and divert your attention in another direction. Tathagata[8] has admonished: "Woman is hindrance to salvation. She is pretentious. She is illusory.""

On the same evening, Kshema had also confessed her deviations in greater details . . .

She said: "That day while venturing into distant villages for begging, I suddenly confronted disciple Upananda on a crossway inside the Sal forest. He had also set out on the same purpose. While moving alongside him through the colossal forest's cool and refreshing cover of shades, I felt as if his warm breaths burnt my cheeks and forehead; I felt as if his amorous proximity rekindled my subdued desire into the flames of an unbridled and rabid sensuousness. The soothing fragrance of his intrepid breath was attractive, enticing; it coiled around me like an intricate and inescapable net, a trammeling incarceration. I was getting ensnared by his captivating glances like a frail pigeon getting entrapped in the surreptitious hunter's deceptively sprawling net. I could hear the ceaseless palpitations of his pulses in the inmost recesses of my barren and shriveled heart. I could feel that his stealthy glances at my half-revealed body were piercing the soft, delicate membranes of my heart like throngs and clusters of acuminous arrows. To resist this attraction, I stayed back and walked behind him."

She continued: "But Upananda told me with a voice of impish instigation: "Being alone in this deep and dense Sal

---

[8] Another name for Lord Buddha.

forest is a painful and discomfiting experience. Isn't it? What deviation of 'dharma' it shall be if we walk together, Kshema?'"

Kshema continued: "Then he held my hand snugly in his and dragged me towards him with some amount of force and virulence; of course, I won't deny that there was a conceivable air of intimacy concealed in that fervent and impeccable force that was overpowering the feebleness of my resistance within moments. An unswerving keenness emanated from his face—a face that had turned red with an exorbitant display of prurience and debauchery sparklingly overflowing across his reddened and ensnaring gaze directed at me, unremittingly. There was insatiable desire crammed in his eyes—eyes that sparkled with the blistering resplendence of uncurbed lustfulness and overflew with the unmitigated rampancy of an expressive and lusty desire. I could well sense that an obnoxious beast had taken possession of him and had vanquished his prudence and more so, he had willfully surrendered to its compelling spells of impetuous carnality. Initially I resisted; but slowly I lost control over my prudence and self-restraint that had till now safeguarded me like a protective cover and contentedly allowed him to drag me closer to his body and explore, willfully, into the dreamy and seductive recesses of my voluptuary body's swarming opulence. His muscles had stiffened with the mad rush of animalistic desire all along; it seemed to me for a moment that I was getting hypnotized by a devilish sorcerer and was lenitively sliding into the tantalizing depths of sorcery and necromancy that he kept weaving around me, unremittingly. But to my utter surprise, there was unbelievable pleasure embedded in that willful captivation; I descended into the shadowy depths of an irresistible frenzy. The soporific smell of his bare, sinewy and muscular torso was delving deeper and deeper into the unexplored expanses of my famished soul; it secretly desired for union. I loved every moment of that inglorious proximity and started relishing the vile and dishonorable sinfulness of this prohibited and amorous togetherness. It seemed as if I was sedated by the contagious air of his inveigling presence and was tranquilized by the inconceivable and bewitching powers of his inexorable captivation. But suddenly I came back to my senses and regained control over my wild, dissipating thoughts."

Kshema told in a choking voice: "Forgive me for that momentary weakness, Acharya. Forgive me."

"Things have gone so far then." Said Acharya Kashyapa, in a rude and unforgiving voice.

Then he continued: "This weakness is not a small mistake, Kshema. It's a horrendous blunder. Fearing this degeneration, one day Tathagata had prohibited women's entry into the community. The fickleness of senses is behind all degeneration. You have to conquer your senses, Kshema. Their vile and annihilative fire of filthy desire shall burn all your long-cherished perseverance towards salvation in a moment, and you shall be reduced to a feculent and abominable beast squalidly riddled with sublunary, carnal desires and abject, lustful rancorousness. That is precisely why Tathagata had instructed the disciples to refrain from the grimy, inexorable appeal of the senses and then only, they could continue to remain relentless pursuers of salvation."

Kshema went away from Acharya Kashyapa in a half-buried, apologetic face.

After this, Kashyapa left for distant places like Pataligrama and Rajagruha for observing some religious performances.

Upananda and Kshema stayed back.

■

Chapter II

It was a beautiful, somnolent afternoon in 'Mahabana Vihara.'

Upananda sat alone inside his room and stared at a mango tree through the window; innumerable newly bloomed buds had pullulated across the tree's intricately stretched-out, messy, and entangled branches. In his weird imagination, Upananda saw a woman's nude and sybaritic limbs lavishly spread out against the mango tree's branches in that languorous and foggy afternoon that was brooding over him like the ineluctable and hypnotic allure of the voluptuous Earth. The tender swell of a low hill at a distance looked to him like a delicate virgin's inflated breast. He was a salvation-seeker and as a principle, must have refrained from such impious, vulgar imaginings that would have driven him unhinderedly into the pestilential darkness of Hell. A herd of Buddhist disciples approached towards his chamber chanting spiritual mantras and listening to them was for Upananda another step closer to salvation. These salvation-seekers usually visited their fellow disciples' rooms in the evening, lighted candles before the statues of Abalokiteswara, Pragyanparamita, Amoghasiddhi, Tara, Akhyoba, Lochana[9] etc. placed therein, and then, roamed from chamber to chamber chanting Lord Buddha's divine mantras, indiscriminately. Today, they did the same.

Upananda looked like getting up from an entrancing reverie. And then he chanted:

---

[9]   These are Buddhist gods and goddesses.

"Buddham Saranam Gachhami,
"Dharmam Saranam Gachhami,
"Sangham Saranam Gachhami."
(I take shelter in Lord Buddha,
I take shelter in the holy religion,
I take shelter in the holy community).

The disciples met Upananda in his room, exchanged a few ritualistic pleasantries, lighted the candles placed below the statues of Abalokiteswara and Pragyanparamita with ghee, paid soulful obeisance to them and left. The ambience got heavier with the smell of burnt ghee and wick and an angelic, divine candour percolated through the air.

But where was the lady whose anklet's jingling symphony Upananda desperately wanted to hear? Where was that paragon of beauty whose dangling silhouette in the air captivated him like a wakeful trance? Where was that sensuous beauty whose titillating image floated before his eyes like an elusive mirage? Where was Kshema—the heavenly beauty that had propelled him towards this forbidden path of transgression?"

"Ah Kshema!" Said Upananda in a slow, indolent and muffled voice. There was a lavish note of intoxication in that voice.

In that ignited moment in a tranquil afternoon, her memory shook Upananda's whole being like a sharp sting of pain. He kept looking into the misty horizon without a blink in his eyes, with the brimming anticipation that Kshema would emerge from there with the stunning clarity of a reverie.

Time passed before his eyes like an uncatchable stream.

Upananda's waiting was prolonged and forbearing; yet, there was no sight of Kshema anywhere around. And then after prolonged waiting on his part, she emerged revealingly from the distant horizon like an unclear silhouette, like a hazy and indistinct apparition slowly precipitating into a gorgeous and dandified woman's figure. Before Upananda, appeared the saffron-attire-clad, the flower-embedded, the slim-figured, the dusky-complexioned, the beautiful Kshema. Her dye-ridden feet looked sumptuously soft, exquisite and colourful whereas her singsong, mellifluous voice was full of a gripping musical symphony. Her slim, supple figure was lascivious, enticing and the curvilinear structure of her tender body captivated Upananda's mind like an inconceivable and tantalizing enigma. The muddled, reddish patches scattered across her silken cheek looked irresistibly winsome and attractive to the dreamily enamoured Upananda who had turned thoroughly enchanted and speechless. Her long stretches of hair elongated almost up to her thin waist resembled a sonorously flowing cascade clung to the hill like a luminescent girdle. Her pair of reddish lips looked to him like the winding reservoirs of a staggering mystery that was entirely undecipherable to the befuddled Upananda. But her half-sunken eyes that resembled inverted lotus leaves were filled with the stoic indifference of a shadowy lake.

Upananda was mesmerized.

Pigeons hooted in the sty while making love. A few disjointed, greyish-white clouds vacillated in the sky like broken petals of a torn-away, dishevelled white rose. The peevish sun winked through them and disappeared like a disinterested celestial passer-by.

With the animating touch of Kshema's deep, mercurial breath hitting against his skin like the gush of an abrupt, stormy wind, Upananda was transported back to his senses, with a sudden and enlivening jerk. He gazed unceasingly for quite some time into the tranquilizing depths of her eyes and was lost in those depths like a forlorn sea-voyager navigating aimlessly through the ocean's endless, bluish, and interminable water-stretch. Kshema's varnished face glowed like the polished visage of some goddess's stone-effigy carved on marble by an adept stone-mason. She looked like preparing to ask a question.

Upananda asked with a soft and considerate voice: "What would you ask me, dear? Please do not hesitate. Ask me without the slightest of inhibitions."

Kshema stretched her right palm towards Upananda and asked in a blushful voice: "Dear Upananda! Can you please look at my palm and prognosticate whether I shall be able to achieve salvation or not?"

Upananda held Kshema's palm in his hands like a hypnotized man. Palm-telling was indeed a prohibited art for the disciples and thus, as a principle, he should have wilfully refrained from entertaining Kshema's illegitimate request. Yet, he kept holding her soft, spongy palm in his hands in that mesmeric afternoon without any fear or compunction of such stringent religious proscriptions. It seemed as if with the enthralling touch of Kshema's pulpy, tinctured hand, his hungry nerves and tendons were rejuvenated with a renewed sensation and vivaciousness. He felt as if his inside-being was filled with a re-energizing vigour and vitality and he wanted to relive his relinquished sensual life again—a life that was lying concealed beneath the camouflaging cover of compulsive, religious self-abnegation. His whole existence seemed to have gotten dissolved in a fathomless vacuum that was looming large on him, like the empty and ever-expansive sky, in that lone, captivating moment. He felt like having achieved salvation in Kshema's mesmeric touch in that dusky, pigeon-infested afternoon—the long-cherished salvation which he didn't achieve so far through steadfast and austere self-abnegation.

"This is the emptiness in which everything dissolves summarily—body and soul, flesh and appearance, everything. This is the touch through which the body transforms into the bodiless; this is the fathomless vacuum into which will converge the virile, exuberant universe of all living beings. This is salvation." Thought Upananda.

For a moment, he spotted the same happiness, the same contentment, and the same exuberance flashing across the faces of Abalokiteswara and Pragyanparamita like momentary glimpses of fire.

---

[10] They are famous Buddhist god and goddess respectively, one male and the other female. In their statues, they are always found meditating while being in deep embrace with each other. Abalokiteswara represents kindness and compassion while Pragyanparamita represents indestructible wisdom.

The warmth of his breath was almost burning Kshema's squishy, delicate palm. She could recognize conceivable traces of carnality effervescing vivaciously through the profusive outpour of his rapid and turbulent breaths. She quietly dragged her palm back from Upananda's hands with downcast eyes and demurely hid it in her attire, while purportedly avoiding frontal eye-contact with him. A faint and implicit expression of shame glimmered capriciously on her lips for a moment and then, vanished into obscurity. Her eyes were closing down beneath her languidly descending brows, as if being inebriated by the fiendish and conjuring spell of lubricity woven on her by Upananda. She was inescapably caught in the interface of two conflicting emotions—whether to resist Upananda's impermissible activities or to wilfully surrender to his tactful and clandestine flirtatiousness? But she asked herself that if she had to resist, then why did she come to him in the first place? She knew quite well that she could not throw Upananda out of her mind. She tried to do that many a times, but did not succeed. Upananda had sufficiently intruded into her subconscious, into the unexplored depths of her rapacious soul, like an imperious and obtrusive trespasser. She had understood that if she resisted him and his spurious advances, then it was nothing but a barefaced lie that she would be telling herself— a sham, a subterfuge. On the other hand, if she wilfully surrendered to his supposititious advances, then it would be nothing but a blatant and outrageous violation of her 'dharma,' a currish blurt on her character—her pure and unblemished character. But she could not resist her temptation for a union with Upananda; it was growing irresistibly bigger and bigger, and snowballing into an expression of ignominious carnality, a primitive and incurable curse.

But somehow, she controlled her emotions and left the place quickly.

After she left, Upananda got back to his senses. But Kshema had disappeared by now. Upananda's wakeful trance was gradually coming to an end in the midst of the pigeons' relentless hooting inside the sty.

He came back into his chamber. The candle below Abalokiteswara and Pragyanparamita's statues had gotten extinguished long before. A thin ray of moonlight had scattered imperceptibly on the chamber's elongated stone-floor. A tattler bird's restless shout in the night sky kept him awake till late in the night. He was mesmerized by the smell of the mango buds.

Upananda remembered an episode once narrated before him by Acharya Kashyapa . . .

*****

That day while returning to his place with his disciples, Tathagata was taking rest in a Sal-forest at the outskirts of the Malla[11] community's village. The euphoric and rapturous joy of spring had copiously spread through the forest like his numinous and heavenly blessing. A cuckoo's thrilling song woke the forest up from its luxuriant slumber while the ceaseless humming of the jungle-bees added to the forests' soulful and enrapturing whine.

At this point, the vulgar thought of women disturbed disciple Ananda's mind who asked Tathagata with all earnestness: "God! What should be the relation between women and the disciples?"

Tathagata answered: "Every disciple's duty is to stay away from women like staying away from venomous snakes."

Ananda asked: "Hey God! But what if some beautiful lady crosses your path, flaunting the enthralling voluptuousness of her body? Will it not ignite your hidden carnality?"

Tathagata answered: "Then you have to control yourself by subduing the fickleness of your senses. That is the whole purpose behind our salvation-seeking endeavours. We have to

---

[11] An ancient Buddhist community.

train ourselves to command our senses, and not to fall, obtusely, into their pretentious and illusory trap. We have to make them our slaves, and not the reverse. And if we allow the reverse to happen then we regressively get reduced to orgiastic and prurient beasts and, nothing else. And the whole salvation-seeking endeavour gets thwarted and nullified in a moment."

Ananda asked again: "Then what will be the relationship between the disciples and women?"

Tathagata answered: "The disciples must refrain from verbal interactions with them."

Ananda asked again: "If a lady starts interacting with a disciple out of her own intriguing volition?"

Tathagata answered: "Then quietly go away from her with a downcast head."

*****

After a few days, Acharya Kashyapa came back from his sojourn from Pataligrama and Rajagruha. In the meantime, the infamous Upananda-Kshema episode was in a way completely obliterated from his mind, particularly due to his many other pressing religious preoccupations. He had thought that it was only a momentary lapse on their part and had anticipated that after that day's volitional repentance, they might have readily mended their ways, and might have expeditiously refined their licentious demeanours. But now he had been listening to unbelievable anecdotes of Upananda and Kshema's unflinching moral transgressions and depravity.

That is why on the next 'Repentance Day,' he was angrily waiting for them like a wounded tiger, ready to pounce on them the moment they arrived, to tear their flesh apart, of course not because of primitive hunger, but for the sheer, ravenous anger burning inside him like inextinguishable fire.

The faint light of dusk had slowly descended on 'Mahabana Vihara.' The exhausted sun, after the whole day's uninterrupted burning, had lost its blistering flames and had fastidiously dipped into the cool, freezing waters of the sea. Its faint, diminishing light had given way to the rampaging darkness of the night that ran amok through its disembodied, skeletal offal like an unpreventable and pervasive blight.

Yet there was no news of Upananda and Kshema.

Acharya Kashyapa was losing his patience.

He waited unwearyingly for a long time, yet they did not arrive. But after some time, only Kshema arrived and there was no Upananda with her. She stood before the Acharya like an exanimate effigy, with a buried head, drooped shoulders and a pair of dismayed eyes; her usually buoyant and vivacious spirit had given way to a dull and somber inertness and her dreary torso looked depressingly crestfallen. Her resplendent eyes had lost their lustrous velvetiness and her low-beating heart seemed to be turgidly impregnated with clusters of unrevealed mysteries. A cold shiver ran through her spine like lightening passing through a lumpy mass of cadaverous dead wood.

Kshema stood before the Acharya timorously while obliviously drawing desultory and arbitrary lines on the ground with her left toe. She had lost the courage and conviction of a pietistic, self-righteous and priggish disciple. She could not look straight and unwaveringly into the Acharya's torrid and conflagrant pair of eyes and interact. An afflictive and penitential feeling of guilt gnawed her inside 'being' like a carnivorous beast.

Acharya Kashyapa hurriedly asked: "I am listening lots of unpleasant things about you and Upananda. Are they true Kshema?"

Kshema answered in an apprehensive voice: "All that you hear might not be true, my lord. But everything that you hear might not be entirely false either."

Kshema was getting wounded by Acharya Kashyapa's incessant bombardment of probing and repugnant questions that pierced into her inside 'being' like ravaging herds of bloodthirsty beasts, lacerated her throbbing torso, extirpated her flesh, nerves and tendons with their sharp-edged, lethal claws and canines.

But Acharya Kashyapa was perhaps deriving some sadistic pleasure from her enforcedly candid confessions. There was no end to his hardnosed interrogation; he went on asking her questions, audaciously, like a hungry and avaricious beast whose desire for flesh had not yet been consummated. Yet, the façade of anger and intolerance on his face was brazenly apparent.

Kshema continued with her repentance: "Another day while we walked together through the Sal forest, one of Upananda's arms surrounded my waist like a curvaceous snake calamitously coiling around the palpitating body of its arrested prey. And then his fingers started caressing across the sublimated region of my fleshy navel-area. Willy-nilly, I mustered some courage and tried to push his bullish and puissant hand away; but it was too strong and sturdy for the frailty of my incapacitated resistance. I could feel traces of indefatigable brute force suffused in his obstreperous hands; and slowly, I lost my vestigial strength and will for resistance. I was rather willfully succumbing to his flagitious advances and it was no more a painful and harrowing experience at all; rather, there was an inexplicable sense of joy in that momentous and impromptu surrender. I could not evade the magnetic allure of his body that smelt of the unctuous odour of the titillating and seductive Earth. This emboldened Upananda even more and his incorrigible, impetuous hands arduously trespassed into the proscribed limits of my verboten nudity. I started cooperating instead of resisting."

Kshema was no more afraid to confess things in a blatant and revealing manner.

Acharya Kashyapa's ascetic, sunken eyes suddenly looked tawdry, flagrant and glittery as if burning in a strange, virulent sensation. From beneath his suppressed senses, an unstoppable spark of prurience flung itself sprightly into his mind like an abrupt, evanescent glint of fire. In his pale, weakened arms he felt the strength and rejuvenation of Upananda's sinewy, muscular body. The waves of animalistic passions rippled through his sanctified body like a ubiquitous and devastating flood. He felt like having touched the voluptuous thigh of some beautiful maiden. His fingers seemed like caressing across that maiden's fleshy and solicitous navel-area. He seemed like losing his self-restraint in that ignited moment infested with intrusive, impious thoughts, but, of course, could amend this momentary lapse with his long-cultivated wisdom and abstemious self-restraint.

Like a possessed being, Kshema went on talking: "I tried my best to control myself, Acharya. I kept praying to Tathagata: "Lord! Give me the resolve, strength and power to evade this chimerical and illusory trap." But I was not able to do that. I rather anxiously waited for these alluring and pleasurable moments with Upananda in some secluded and cloistered precinct inside that dark and sibylline the Sal-jungle. I had secretively started enjoying his bewitching proximity. I do not know how my pious and reticent mind got so much distracted and deviated."

Acharya Kashyapa shouted like a lion: "You will go to Abhichi Hell, you sinner." The surmounting expressions of unbearable wrath and disdain on his face looked awfully emphatic, clear and abounding. But, of course, Kshema could readily spot the inordinate façade of artificiality in that impromptu explosion of temper.

She could spot envy in the Acharya's eyes. The salaciousness of her confessions had reignited his coveted sexual desire towards an untenable and spontaneous outburst. But she knew that the Acharya had cultivated enough self-control through years of prolonged perseverance to brutally subdue such abrupt flare-ups of recalcitrant, sublunary passions.

She told again in a tearful voice: "But Acharya! Somebody is dragging me into this filthy quagmire of sensuality against my conscious will."

"That is nothing but your ill will." Said Acharya Kashyapa.

"But who gave me that ill will?" Asked Kshema.

Acharya Kashyapa said: "Your filthy mind."

"But who disturbed my mind?" Asked Kshema again.

Acharya Kashyapa said: "Your senses."

Then there was a complete, breathtaking silence that prevailed between the two. Kshema did not have any further question to ask the Acharya, neither did the latter have anything to curse Kshema for. But in reality, her proximity was both a pleasurable and tormenting experience for him. His composite 'being' was getting cleaved into two oppositional halves—one that stunk of filthy and ignoble carnality and the other that overflew with calm and sublime self-restraint. The Acharya was caught in a terrible fix, an imbroglio, an awful discomfiture which he hardly had confronted before. But he regained his composure with an unassailable stroke of abstinence.

But there was no trace of Upananda till now in that area.

Perhaps he won't come. These days he hardly came for the 'Repentance Days.'

But the Acharya did not understand why an austere and principle-abiding disciple like Upananda chose the path of transgression so abruptly? He kept pondering over it and couldn't find an answer. The frowns on his sunken forehead became curvier and harder. He thought that Upananda and Kshema had become threats to the community's longstanding sanctimony and grandeur. And if they were not thrown away from 'Mahabana Vihara,' then the principle-based decorum of the institution would crumble to pieces. Thinking about it, the quietude and serenity of his saintly mind were getting thoroughly bollixed into multiple strands of divergent, confounding and unsettling thoughts. But before the stern, disciplinary action was initiated, he wanted to see them making love, at least once.

But O God! What strange proclivity was it on his part! What an absurd desire was it for a man who had mastered exemplary self-restraint through prolonged and inexpugnable perseverance! Why did he contemplate to see them making love?

To satisfy the ephemeral fickleness of his senses? To reignite the squalid passions that he had vanquished and subdued so far? To re-enliven the slaughtered demons in his blood? To bring out the filthy beasts hibernating beneath his pacified nerves? Acharya Kashyapa was asking these questions to himself in tranquility.

Breaking the silence, he asked Kshema: "Is this your everyday business, Kshema? This prohibited relationship?"

Kshema did not say anything out of shame. She kept quiet.

Yes, this had turned into an everyday business. Each day, Kshema's feet compulsively dragged her towards the Sal jungle on Sadanira's banks where Upananda waited patiently for her with unblinking, fidgety eyes. Kshema appeared before him piercing the condensed veil of creepers and leaves of that mysterious, opaque and impenetrable forest. With her attractive and dandified attire, she looked enchanting, subduing, pulchritudinous . . . She dazzled before Upananda like a glimmering apparition of the veiled, cryptic and sensuous forest itself that engulfed its indwellers with its arcane and apocryphal spells of witchery and pederasty. Upananda looked straight into Kshema's eyes; she blushed. A sudden, fugacious flicker of smile sparkled on her velvety lips for a moment and then vanished into the forest's abounding darkness, like a tiny, flirtatious and uncatchable little bird. Upananda felt a strange and mystifying virulence in his nerves and made calculated advances towards her. She feigned resistance the artificiality of which was irrefutably evident. Upananda dragged her onto himself and Kshema could feel an invigorating rush of maddening desire traversing across her spine with the speed of lightning. There was an inconceivable design carved in his magic touch.

Slowly, Upananda undressed her with scanty resistance from the latter. Upananda filled her body with infinite kisses. He felt the softness of her breasts deep inside the secret coves of his tormented heart. Kshema's denuded body was flooded with his rapid and turbulent breaths that traversed across her stripped and bare-skinned soft torso like the shifting waves of a plundering storm. They merged into each other's hungry bodies and penetrated deep into the infinite recesses of their craven souls. Their bared bodies sparked like gold in the verdant moonlit night that had turned notoriously glossy and sensuous with their exorbitant display of amorousness. In that mesmeric moment of togetherness, they had lost their consciousness to the extent that they remained unaware of the passing, noiseless stream of time.

The vagrant moon roved across the sky like a celestial eavesdropper. The sweet symphony of a flute came floating from some distant tribal cottage and enwrapped their denuded bodies like a thin, pellucid, mantle. Upananda and Kshema got up, and sat on the moon-blanched sand and washed their bodies with the translucent shower of moonlight filtering through the clumsy and embroidered network of branches and leaves spread out against the crimson sky like intricate traceries carved on a colourful canopy. Kshema buried her face on Upananda's shoulder.

In those hypnotic moments of union, they didn't see a thing around, not even Acharya Kashyapa who stood behind them like a dark, sinister presence.

They did not know how long the Acharya had been observing them. It was beyond their imagination that he would be there to observe their proximity, so keenly and iniquitously, in the adumbrating darkness of that sinful night. They were still in deep embrace with their unclothed bodies clung to each other like inseparable shadows. There was no other sound than that of River Sadanira's jubilant, dancing waves, the slow, maddening rustle of the Sal trees' leaves and the thrilling symphony from a distant flute.

There was silence everywhere.

In Acharya Kashyapa's thundering voice, the tranquilized forest started trembling like a palm frond in wintry rain. He shouted: "Upananda! Kshema!"

The Acharya's voice almost choked inside his throat when he lambasted vociferously at the blasphemous duo. In anger and hatred, he was trembling like a feats-patient. The community's degeneration was stupendously visible to him like the bared and risible pages of an open book. The complete and thoroughgoing annihilation of 'dharma' was not far away.

Upananda and Kshema stood dumbfounded before him. Kshema had lost her consciousness in craven terror that had seized her petrified inner 'being' like a paranormal trauma. She came to her senses and they dressed themselves up within moments.

But Upananda was doggedly frigid, callous and dauntless in an ornery display of his characteristic nonchalance and temerity. He continued to remain unwaveringly stubborn and unyielding, and looked straight into the Acharya's eyes with the sinister conviction of a pigheaded and unconcerned sinner. He remained thoroughly unapologetic.

Acharya Kashyapa told in a grave voice: "Upananda! Kshema! You have become slaves of your senses and have violated the principles of 'dharma.' You are no more claimants of salvation; you have no other place than the Abhichi Hell to go. I am giving you curse. You are dispelled from the community, with immediate effect, right now. Life is transient; the senses are illusory. You forgot this great teaching of Tathagata in your mindless surrender to the attraction of the body. You no more deserve the right to remain in the community."

Upananda asked in a calm and unruffled voice: "O Lord! If life is a lie, then how could salvation be truth? Is it not an illusion again?"

Acharya Kashyapa was left speechless. He did not have an immediate answer to Upananda's question whose validity, nevertheless, could not have been entirely discounted. He left angrily thumping his feet thunderously on the ground.

After the Acharya left, Upananda and Kshema dissolved in the Sal forest like two home-returning herons dissolving imperceptibly in the frosted horizon. They had no place in 'Mahabana Vihara.' Before them, there were the inviting dark depths of the forest and an uncertain path that led them pell-mell into the shadowy depths of a mystic and unforeseen labyrinth. They kept walking through the forest while the faint and inaudible sound of their moving feet drowned in the former's abstruse and cryptic silence that readily engulfed every little commotion around like a quiet, ravenous and invisible monster. They walked listening to a flute's symphony that led them towards a distant tribal village where they thought they could spend the night.

The whole of Baisali had become a godforsaken place for them. Acharya Kashyapa's punishment had been formally authenticated by the community through a massive and unambiguous referendum. They were no more offered food in the hosts' houses. Wherever they went begging for food, they confronted dirty banters and sarcasms mercilessly thrown at them from the callous and aversive masses of caustic and contemptuous common populace. The news of their expulsion from the community had spread through the kingdom like unstoppable wildfire.

Tortured by extreme hunger and shame, Upananda and Kshema kept walking towards Magadha. They fed themselves with the fruits of the jungle and drank water from the streams. In exhaustion, their bodies were giving away. The raising dust from the road had made their torsos look dirty, pale and haggard. But yet, they were not sad and remorseful about their past; rather a keen and mutually comforting proximity had enlivened them into the vigours of a new, luxuriant sensation. By revolting against the incarcerations of 'dharma,' they had become harbingers of another life, of another existence. They had denounced self-restraint and had willfully surrendered to their instinct and their destiny. There was momentous freedom and ecstasy in that surrender.

One day while roaming through the forest, they heard a prowling tiger's ferocious roar from inside a leaf-crowded, thickened haze somewhere around and clasped each other in surmounting fear. They stood dumbfounded, and thought that their deep embrace was indeed their protection against the fear of the tiger and its menacing approach. They had perhaps not embraced each other so tightly before, not even in those intimate moments of fervid, carnal proximity on the sprawling sand of river Sadanira. Yet, the intimidation of imminent death lurking threateningly around carved in their eyes bulging expressions of terror and sent shifting waves of fast-moving tremor across their shivering bones, stiffening their nerves with impending, craven trepidation. The consternation of imminent death had frozen their limbs into inaction. The tiger's roar reverberated through the forest like death's cruel and internecine laughter; they trembled in pernicious terror.

They didn't know how long they had stood there frozen, flabbergasted. But there was no dirty vulgarism in that embrace; neither was there any remorseful feeling of impermissible sexual intimacy in them. Like two placid stone effigies, they stood there embracing each other in gripping fear that had amalgamated them into one, conjugated whole. Kshema had cuddled Upananda tightly in his arms, whereas he had pressed his head inadvertently against her pliant breasts.

But suddenly they were woken up by somebody's crude and intimidating laughter in that abyssal and impervious forest. The laughter spread through the forest like a volcanic tremor passing ferociously through the skeletal body of the dazed Earth. For a moment it seemed to be some ghost's or of some mysterious creature of that enigmatic forest; but they quickly realized that it was indeed a human being's laughter. Upananda and Kshema looked all around in curiosity and found at a distance a strange creature squatting leisurely inside a tangled mess of creepers, while throwing strange, curious and investigative waves of glances at them. That creature looked like a wild man who was stark nude though his whole body was enshrouded by long braids of hair cascading him from head to toe. He had a magnificent pair of wide and provocative eyes which however did not bear even the closest resemblance to any kind of cruelty or viciousness. Rather, Upananda and

Kshema saw that those eyes looked tender, munificent and considerate.

But they did not understand why that monk laughed so loudly and boisterously at them. They surmised that perhaps there was some unrevealed mystery behind that prolonged and inexplicable laughter.

It was an Ajivika monk. He accosted Upananda and Kshema with courteous gestures to come near him.

By now the tiger's roar had stopped and the forest had become grievously silent.

Upananda and Kshema had been thoroughly exhausted because of extreme hunger. Willy-nilly, they started approaching towards that monk's groove, while at the same time, measuring each of their steps with utter care and cautiousness as if they were apprehensive of some unknown danger lurking around. Kshema was particularly frightened by the monk's awfully obnoxious look and strange demeanour and was unwilling to move further at all. Upananda however instilled some confidence into her terrified psyche by saying: "Don't worry Kshema. This man is an Ajivika monk. These are bizarre and strange creatures, as you see. During his sojourn towards River Niranjana for the ultimate attainment of nirvana, Lord Buddha had stayed with this community for a short duration. These people are hugely destiny-believers, you know. The Lord left this community after a while since he could not reconcile to their libertine belief-systems and could not approve of their unfettered, renegade, and bohemian lifestyle. These people stay naked all the time, as you see. Their long braids of hair are their only attire. Their prophet Ajitha Keshakambali also lived like this.

With Upananda's encouraging words, Kshema felt a little reassured and moved closer to the monk's groove along with Upananda even though her steps were still cagey and apprehensive and her cautious face still elicited a glimmering expression of vigilance and suspiciousness. Ajivika accosted them with a tender and mellifluous voice and said: "Folks! You need not fear me. Come here. It's all the game of destiny. It was predestined that we would meet here."

He gave them some fruits to eat. They felt a little comforted after eating them. But they did not know how to initiate a conversation with this strange and bizarre-looking monk.

Ajivika asked: "Perhaps you two are the ousted disciples of 'Mahabana Vihara,' right? Otherwise, how would you be roaming inside this forest like this? But why are you moving like lunatics inside this enigmatic forest? There are savage beasts prowling around and they may devour you within no time."

After a few moments of breathtaking silence, the monk said again: "Perhaps you have been thrown out of your community, right?"

And he quickly knew that his conjecture was absolutely correct.

But there was not even an iota of hatred in the Ajivika monk's expressions. Rather a soothing kindness emanated from his eyes for these two distressed beings.

Upananda mustered some courage and asked: "But why did you laugh so loudly at us in our terrible moments of pain and misery?"

Ajivika prodded Kshema with his finger and told: "Why don't you answer to his question, disciple?"

Kshema shrunk in embarrassment and went a step back and stared at Ajivika with dumbfounded expressions.

Upananda was also absolutely quiet.

The Ajivika monk asked again: "Why did you two stand there in deep embrace near the tree?"

Kshema answered: "Out of fear for our life after listening to the tiger's roar nearby!"

Upananda said: "It was a spontaneous reaction on our part sensing imminent death lurking so near us. We had no other intention. But what made you laugh so loudly at us?"

The Ajivika monk answered: "Of course it is true that I

laughed loudly looking at you. But it was not indeed intended at you two."

Kshema asked: "Then for whom was your laughter intended?"

But instead of answering the question, Ajivika asked a counter question: "Then is it so that human instinct is more powerful than his perseverance, his devotion to 'dharma'?"

Upananda answered: "Well! Your loud and insensitive laughter at us proves that."

A complete silence prevailed again, except the restive twitter of birds and the ceaseless singing of the crickets.

Upananda broke the silence and asked: "Then were you laughing at Lord Buddha and his principles? If yes, why?"

The Ajivika monk, instead of answering, again asked a counter question: "What pain did you feel while embracing each other when you were integral parts of your community?"

Upananda and Kshema were completely taken aback by Ajivika's question: "How could he know such things? Is this Ajivika monk omnipresent?" They started asking themselves and looked at each other in an air amazed stupefaction.

The Ajivika monk said smilingly: "That was also an instinctive thing, right!"

Upananda and Kshema did not utter a single word.

Yes! It was their irrepressible instinct that brought them together on Sadanira's banks. How could they have refuted that?

The Ajivika monk said again: "Your instinct overpowered your intellect, your principles of 'dharma,' right?"

Upananda and Kshema answered unequivocally: "Yes!"

The Ajivika monk said: "That is why I was laughing loudly, at Lord Buddha and his futile indoctrinations to humankind about self-abnegation being the only pathway towards the attainment of salvation. Being such an enlightened soul, he could not comprehend the fundamental truth that all principles crumble before human instinct just like a sandbank crumbles before a devastating flood. Instinct is natural and is an innate human attribute that accompanies him from his birth to death whereas self-abnegation is artificial, concocted and meaningless and is forcibly imposed on him like a redundant and superfluous encumbrance. Compulsive self-abnegation is not the sanctified boulevard leading to the sacred arena of salvation. If that was the case, then oxen could have attained salvation by being celibates. Acharya Keshakambali[12] has said and has said it emphatically that merely tonsuring your head will not lead you towards the attainment of salvation. That is why I was laughing at Lord Buddha and his unexplainable inanity and foolishness so far as his comprehension of the basic human instinct is concerned. I wonder how can his understanding of the fundamental texture of human nature be so faulty and fragile? I wonder how such an enlightened mind could remain so awfully oblivious towards an efficacious cognition of the very foundational attributes of human 'self' and human psychology? How could he fail so miserably to comprehend that self-abnegation is a mere mask to camouflage human instinct? The moment that mask falls, the latter comes to the fore and reigns supreme. Lord Buddha could not comprehend that self-abnegation is copiously illusory and pretentious. He did not understand that the only truth is destiny."

The whole forest trembled with another peal of laughter from Ajivika.

Upananda and Kshema bid adieu to him and started moving towards Magadha. Pataligrama was still a long way. Following them was Ajivika's cavorting laughter, like an imperceptible ghost.

■

---

[12] One of the prophets of the Ajivika community.

Chapter III

One day elderly guru Upali came to visit 'Mahabana Vihara.' He had received prior information about Upananda and Kshema's disgraceful ouster from the community; the news had struck him like a sudden and frightful flash of lightening, and he was thoroughly rattled from inside. It was beyond his wildest comprehension to hear such unsettling and disgraceful news, particularly in a scenario when he had adequately known Upananda and Kshema as two pious, dedicated and principle-abiding disciples. He couldn't believe that such a resilient, principle-based religion of theirs would meet such blatant and inglorious violations so quickly.

But it was not just Baisali from where such violations were getting reported; such stories poured in indiscriminately from other regions of the kingdom as well. But of course, Baisali's Bajjiputtas[13] were a little unruly and truculent in these matters right from the beginning; their repeated violations of 'dharma' and its principles were a usual and recurring phenomenon in the community. So, Upananda and Kshema's insolent transgressions were perhaps not entirely implausible in this scenario, particularly considering the fact that they were after all the progenies of this mordant, whimsical and heretical race.

Upali was one amongst the religion's earliest disciples. After Gautama's favourite disciples Ananda and Rebata, he enjoyed the highest veneration in the community as a

---

[13] An ancient community in Baisali.

steadfast practitioner of the religion's obdurate and binding principles. Before his death, Ananda had bestowed the community's stewardship on Upali reposing tremendous faith in the latter's ability to be able to maintain the religion's principle-based decorum with utmost dedication and steadfastness. And he had instructed him, before his demise, that he must ensure that Lord Buddha's Ten Commandments were observed with absolute perfection and trenchant inviolability. In other words, the community's future depended on Upali and the other senior-most gurus who could exercise stringent austerity in terms of the strict observance of 'dharma.'

But how could he have handled this newly developing recklessness and indiscipline in the community? He didn't know how to deal with these new disciples who had surrendered themselves to the temptations of evil and had started worshipping the sinister forces reigning supreme in their besmirched hearts. This was, of course, a fresh and undesirable development.

Interestingly however, even Lord Buddha was not so rigid and unforgiving in his principles. He did understand that there are sublunary human fallibilities afflicting every human being and no individual, however pious, resilient and principle-abiding he may be, is entirely immune to them. Thus, he used to forgive the violators of 'dharma' and perpetrators of sin with a magnanimous heart. He was a true humanist.

*****

It was an event before Lord Buddha's demise.

The Lord, while moving from Baisali to Kushinagar for the last time, took rest in host Kunda's house in village Paba. Kunda offered him pork in supper eating which the Lord fell terminally ill. In such a dire situation, he didn't know whether he would reach Kushinagar or not. In a way, he was preparing for his 'parinirvana.'

It was the sprawling Sal forest on the banks of river

Hiranyabati. Disciple Ananda prepared a bed made of broken twigs and scattered leaves for him in that jungle.

It was late in that night. Tathagata's final moments were approaching.

Ananda asked: "O Lord! Who shall be our guru after you? Who will guide us towards salvation?"

"Dharma." Answered Tathagata.

Ananda asked: "O Lord! Will it be possible for the disciples to observe all the strict principles of 'dharma'?

Tathagata answered in a faint voice: "If in future you find some of them to be too rigid and ostentatious, you can amend them through referendum."

Tathagata was a thoroughgoing rationalist. He knew quite well that in a continually transitioning society, no principle can remain permanent and unaltered. With the changing time, some of them have to be altered or at least modified. Otherwise, time will abdicate them and they won't survive its sweeping onslaught.

But after Tathagata's demise, the disciples institutionalized his principles as rigid and inviolable norms. Of course, it used to be a common practice to save any 'dharma' from degradation.

But wherever there is an unwarranted imposition of rigidity, there is also found its gross and manifest violation. Every prophet's devised paths have met similar consequences, without any doubt. Irrational inflexibility in the name of strict observation of 'dharma' has ultimately resulted in its own violation and infringement.

After Gautama Buddha's demise, the religion had confronted similar consequences.

Older gurus like Upali, though highly respected in the community, were nearing the hundredth years of their lives. Some of them had also surpassed one hundred years. In this scenario where this sacred religion was passing through a transitional phase, legion, aberrant younger disciples started entering into the community's pious and ensconced premises in the attraction of simple and uncomplicated living and delicious food in the hosts' houses. As a religion, Buddhism was becoming increasingly popular and reverential amongst the common masses who held this religion in high esteem and worshipped Lord Buddha as their indubitable savior and messiah. However, the new entrants exhibited multiple lapses in the observance of 'dharma.' How could this aberrant bunch of pleasure-seeking young folks have behaved in a scrupulous and restrained manner like Lord Buddha himself?

Upali that day remembered the episode involving disciple Subhada in the Sal jungle. Lord Buddha hardly delivered sermons to a young disciple out of his own volition. But that day God only knew what he saw in Subhada, he preached him lots of sermons with immense interest and enthusiasm. But when the news of his demise spread through the community, Subhada was spotted on the streets of Baisali dancing and reveling with a joyous and celebratory demeanour; he was shouting vociferously: "It's great that Buddha has passed away and has attained his long-awaited 'parinirvana.' Now there will be nobody to dictate terms to us in the community, to tell us what to do and what not to do. We are now free birds. We will enjoy life to the full, as per our buoyant and libertine whims and fancies."

But ironically, many thought that it is because of the insurmountable grief that has captivated Subhada due to the Lord's tragic demise, he has lost his sanity and is behaving in a strange, bizarre and devious manner. They prayed to the Buddha for his speedy recovery. But Ananda knew quite well then that it was indeed the beginning of a disaster, a catastrophe that was very soon going to snowball into a cataclysmic apocalypse and devour their holy religion with its all-encompassing, fiery, diabolic tongue.

Both Ananda and Upali had understood the gravity of the scenario. They tried their best to restore order and discipline in the community.

It's a fact that nobody had written down Tathagata's sermons anywhere. During his lifetime, they were orally transmitted from mouth to mouth and were solemnly observed as sacrosanct rules. But how could the new and younger disciples have comprehended the intrinsic values embedded in those sermons, and how could they have unquestioningly accepted them as the sole guiding principles of their religious lives? They had never seen in their own eyes Lord Buddha delivering those sermons to his disciples. They had only listened them from the older gurus who claimed to have heard them directly from the Lord when he was alive. But could the older gurus' words have been taken at face value? The sermons might have undergone weird distortions while passing from mouth to mouth, from generation to generation, and from community to community. On this matter, the younger disciples had turned thoroughly repellent and non-conforming. They had become unruly and deviant.

But to stop such degeneration of 'dharma,' Upali had arranged the first Buddhist conference in Rajagruha, almost immediately after Lord Buddha's 'parinirvana.'

In that conference, the older gurus who had presumably heard Lord Buddha directly, recited his sermons from their memory. A total of eighty-four thousand sermons were recited. Complied together, they were named as *Tripitaka* which later was unanimously accepted as the holy Buddhist scripture.

Ananda was gleefully assured that after Buddha's sermons were meticulously written down, they could never have been violated. But they had no idea that day that they were trying to stop a flooding river with a mere sandbank.

Buddha's sermons were also known as 'Binayas' and 'Sutras.'[14] But the new disciples kept on questioning their authenticity as being Lord Buddha's own said words.

And truly, there was no solution to this mess. The older gurus felt helpless and dejected.

Upali also observed that the indiscipline had escalated with the entry of female disciples into the community. The male

---

[14] They are the constituent parts of the holy Buddhist scripture *Tripitaka*.

disciples had started openly enjoying their company without any shame or compunction. There was licentiousness in the air. Upali thought that if the Lord did not rescue the community from heaven, then how could they do the same? It was clearly beyond their sublunary powers.

Another anecdote floated in Upali's memory. It was an event during Tathagata's living days, in Baisali's 'Mahabana Vihara.'

Gautama's adoptive mother Gautami Prajapati approached the Lord with an earnest plea: "Son! After your biological mother's death, I am the one who have raised you like my own son. You were my only hope. But now you have relinquished the world and have become famous as Buddha, leaving me alone and destitute. I have no shelter, no hope. You adopt me into your community and let me live in peace in your vicinity for the rest of my life."

It was the ardent plea of a lone, destitute mother to her son.

But the usually kind-hearted Buddha had mercilessly rejected Gautami's plea that day and had categorically declined to accept her in the community. Gautami made her plea three times. Every time, it was rejected hard-heartedly by the Lord.

But Gautama Buddha could never discard his favourite disciple Ananda's plea. Knowing this, Gautami went to Ananda and requested him to present her case before the Lord on her behalf.

When Ananda presented Gautami's plea before Tathagata, the Lord emitted a deep, and prolonged sigh of helplessness and said: "Ananda! I am not going to live long. The protection of the community is now your sole responsibility. How can I refuse your supplications?"

Then the Lord paused for a moment and said: "But don't forget Ananda that the way the ravenous throngs of locusts decimate the corn field in a few moments, women would do the same to the community once they are given entry to its sanctified and ensconced premises. You shall see that the religion introduced by me that would have easily survived for ten thousand years will now survive only for one thousand years."

Upali thought that Gautama's words were now going to be very true. Let alone one thousand years, the religion was perhaps not going to survive for even one hundred years.

But how could he now have resisted the deterioration?

The 'Binayas' and the 'Sutras' were written down with utmost care and precision. But now the news of their daily, systematic violation tormented Upali's heart to a great extent while at the same time, his incapacity to counteract with immediacy and vehemence was gnawing his conscience and decimating his ego with excruciating pain and exasperation.

In the meanwhile, guru Yasha came to meet Upali after receiving the news of his arrival and presence in 'Mahabana Vihara.'

Yasha sat on a mat and without wasting any time, said: "Great Upali! The community is on the path of absolute destruction. Do you know that?"

Upali asked in a depressed and panic-stricken voice: "Why do you say so, Yasha."

Yasha answered: "I hear frequently that the disciples in 'Mathura Vihara' no more follow the instructions of 'dharma.' I once went to there to ascertain the veracity of these complaints and to ensure whether such impunities are indeed in occurrence or are falsely implicated? You won't believe guru Upali that the younger disciples have started eating salt along with food—a thing that was strictly prohibited by Tathagata. Is it not a sign of imminent destruction?"

Upali asked in a worried voice: "What else did you observe, Yasha?"

Yasha had painfully witnessed lots of indiscipline and infringement of 'dharma' in 'Mathura Vihara.' He would not have believed them unless he witnessed them in his own eyes; the infringements were so blatant and outrageous that he felt an inhibition to narrate them verbatim in a sacred guru's presence. He also knew how these anecdotes would hurt Upali's pious sentiment deeply, and irretrievably.

But somehow he made up his mind not to fruitlessly camouflage such infringements and decided to keep Upali abreast of the recent violations of 'dharma' in the community. He started describing the story of Chandrakirti in 'Mathura Vihara.'

That day a drunken Chandrakirti invited a few other disciples to drink liquor with him, in a congregated companionship.

One disciple resisted: "Tathagata has prohibited liquor for disciples."

Chandrakirti answered in a drunken voice: "Yes! Tathagata never drank liquor. But if he drank it once, he would have never prohibited it for others."

Then he started laughing boisterously in an obscene, vulgar and offensive manner.

Yasha watched Chandrakirti's misdemeanour from a distance. A thing like this in the Buddhist premises was unthinkable for him.

Another disciple said in a toughened and resistant voice: "But drinking liquor is a violation of the Buddhist principles, Chandrakirti."

Chandrakirti again answered in a drunken voice: "Is there any cognizable violation of principle in drinking fruit juice, dear?"

Some disciples answered in a united voice: "No! It never is."

Chandrakirti asked again: "Then what is the difference between fruit juice and date-palm-juice from which liquor is made? This is nothing but fruit juice."

"No! It's polluted." Said one of the disciples.

Chandrakirti argued: "The curd that the disciples have started drinking is nothing but the rotten form of milk. Eating rotten milk does not become a hindrance to salvation. Then how can rotten fruit juice become a hindrance for the same?"

The disciples who till now were expeditiously confronting and opposing Chandrakirti's brazen and impudent drunkenness kept quiet, being overwhelmed by his irrefutable logic and argument. They could not discover another strain of logic to contest, confront and dismantle Chandrakirti's. On the contrary, thoroughly convinced by his reasoning, they scuffled amongst themselves to drink liquor from the earthen pot and in that noisy altercation, the pot fell down and broke into multiple splinters scattered on the ground. The whole atmosphere became contaminated in the pungent and malodorous smell of the rotten date-palm-juice.

Yasha could not tolerate the unwholesome fracas anymore. He rushed to these deranged disciples to stop them from such unholy indulgences. But the drunken disciples shamelessly invited him from a distance to join them while displaying at him a flurry of vulgar taunts and sarcasms. Deeply humiliated, Yasha went back into his abode with a sad and dejected heart.

That evening, Yasha sermonized the young male and female disciples of 'Mathura Vihara' about the importance of observing Gautama Buddha's commandments. He gave them the instance of Gautama's exemplary renunciation of the attraction of his senses and even, the affection of his mother. Though the disciples listened to his elucidations with discipline and forbearance, they hardly looked like being touched, convinced and influenced by his exhortations. Rather, Chandrakirti counter-argued that if Gautama after achieving salvation could consume victuals from the hands of his disciple's daughter Sujata, then what was the harm in eating a pinch of salt with food or in drinking a bit of the alcoholic date-palm-juice?

Yasha told Upali: "You know Upali! I heard a few disciples in Baisali say that Gautama after his 'parinirvana,' has not ascended to heaven, but rather is stuck somewhere in the limbo from where he keeps sending 'Bodhisattvas' onto Earth to be the saviours of tormented humanity; these 'Bodhisattvas,' in their fabricated parlance, are indeed the fragmentary reincarnations of the Lord himself."

Upali couldn't believe his ears. The hearsay that Gautama Buddha was stuck like a Trishanku[15] in the limbo instead of ascending to Heaven seemed strange, bizarre and unacceptable to him. He thought it was nothing but a fabricated story, a manufactured propaganda to defame the Lord.

Upali asked: "Why then the Lord is stuck in the midway instead of going to the Heaven?"

Yasha said: "These deviant bunch of disciples are spreading the misinformation that we are selfishly concerned about our own individual salvation. We are not bothered about the other living beings in general, about their liberation. That is why Lord Buddha is staying in the limbo and is sending 'Bodhisattva's[16] to Earth to rescue us from blasphemy and damnation of this filthy, sublunary earthly existence. Now Lord Buddha would continue staying in that limbo and would keep sending 'Bodhisattva's to Earth as our saviours and messiahs. They will be our gurus and will lead us to liberation, to salvation."

Upali did not understand any of these newfangled postulations and propagandas.

He counter-argued: "But Lord Buddha had repeatedly advocated for individual salvation. This, in turn, implies that every human being can strive for salvation through his own pursuance and perseverance, purely at an individual level. He only can be his own saviour. What is then the rationale behind this absurd and newfangled indoctrination that the Lord will stay suspended in the limbo and send Bodhisattvas to Earth to rescue its living beings?"

Yasha said: "I simply do not comprehend this

---

[15] A character in Hindu mythology who was stuck in the limbo between Earth and Heaven without really being able to go to any of them.
[16] In Buddhism, a Bodhisattva is a person who is on the path towards Buddhahood and who would propagate the holy values and principles of Buddhism as was done by Lord Buddha himself.

preposterously invented notion of Bodhisattvas. Buddha never believed in the concepts of soul and rebirth. But for some strange and inexplicable reason, these younger disciples have started advocating the notion of rebirth and have started pontificating that taking rebirth, again and again, is the metaphysical foundation of our existence in this universe inevitably entangled in the cycle of birth, death and rebirth. Further, they have also started studying horoscopes inside the community. Can you believe that Upali? The service rendered towards humanity by the Buddha in his previous births is being narrated by these people in an exaggerated and extravagant manner. The other disciples have started appreciating such stories and absurd inventions, wholeheartedly."

Upali had never imagined that within just one hundred years of Buddha's 'parinirvana,' the religion shall meet such dire consequences. The changing times had implanted lots of bizarre absurdities in the filthy and corrupted minds of these impious, deranged bunches of disciples. If this continued for some more time, unchecked and un-prevented, then the end of the religion was imminent and inevitable. Upali had little doubt about that.

He contemplated for a moment that the sense-enslaved, destiny-believing followers of Charbak[17] whom Buddha had banished from the Jambu Island[18] have now taken rebirth to avenge him and his religion. He asked himself: "What can we do about it, really?"

Yasha answered: "We have to become more proactive and now, in this rarefied and calamitous scenario. After Tathagata's demise a few years ago, the religion became helplessly exposed to lots of deviation and recalcitrance in the hands of the inrushing herds of deviant, licentious disciples into the religion

---

[17] The pioneer of an ancient school of philosophy that believed that the fulfillment of bodily and materialistic desire, and not spiritual self-abnegation, is the pathway to salvation. Charbak and his followers were apostates, in a certain sense.

[18] Refers to the Indian subcontinent.

and to counter that, the first Buddhist conference was arranged in Rajagruha. In this congregation, disciples recited sermons in the presence of Buddha's favourite disciple Ananda. Nearly seven hundred disciples were present in that conference. But this time we have to call for another such congregation to protect our community; the disciples are to be summoned from every side, from every direction—east, west, south and north. We cannot sit quietly submerged in futile inaction. To protect our morally deteriorating religion, we have to confront these unruly bunches of aberrant and ignominious disciples head-on and incarcerate them in the chains of principle and discipline before they could inflict some real, serious and irreparable damage on this beloved religion of ours."

It was decided, unanimously, that Yasha and a few other senior gurus will sojourn to public states like Koshala, Abanti, Mathura, Magadha, Kuru and Panchala and gather gurus and disciples for a large congregation, a mega-conference, an unprecedented religious extravaganza. There they will confront the young, deviant disciples for the last time, and train, command and subdue them with discipline, with regulation and with inviolable orderliness. And this shall be their last attempt to rescue the religion from utmost annihilation.

Upali asked: "But where this conference shall be arranged?"

Yasha answered: "In the same Baisali where the deviations have started!"

Chapter IV

After getting atrociously ousted from 'Mahabana Vihara,' Upananda and Kshema were now two unshackled cranes traversing freely across the limitless firmament of the panoptic, all-embracing sky. They did not have a nest, neither did they have any shelter nor any bondage. They were free birds. Liberated from all religious confinements, they were now set to explore the unbounded plentitude of their youth with bounteous freedom and sovereignty. They had spread their lofty wings flapping indiscriminately across the vast expanses of the spread-out sky and had started plunging into the illimitable excesses of its seductive space.

It was a shining moonlit night.

After a whole day's exhaustion, Upananda and Kshema had taken shelter in a hill's abandoned groove. They quietly listened to the slow, rustling murmur of a brook that ran zigzag through an absurd and muddled congregation of rocks. The sound was low, monotonous and persistent, like the unstoppable beating of their hearts. As the evening gently surrendered to the approaching night, an incredible swirl of white mist rose from the river's lush body like an immense surge of hope. The exhausted moon, bent over the forest, seemed to seek the Earth's infinite repose like a wandering lover who had finally returned to take rest in his beloved's comfort-giving and reposeful breasts. Above the amorphous darkness of the forest, the treetops rose with their spread-out boughs scattered against the dark canvass of the pale sky, like shards of the cleaved night floating disorderedly on the gushing streams of moonbeams.

Upananda and Kshema . . . The earliest beings of Earth . . .

The burning moon of the full-moon-night had brightened the dark, dungeon of that groove with its lavish profusion of light.

Upananda slept luxuriously placing his head on Kshema's lap. He thoroughly enjoyed the sweetness of her proximity.

Breaking the forest's comatose silence, Kshema asked: "Where are we heading Upananda?"

Upananda dragged Kshema closer to his body. Kshema's luxuriant breasts pressed against his forehead flared up his hidden prurience a thousand times more. In silence, they burnt in the fire of seductive carnality while Kshema lowered her face towards Upananda's and kissed him, with the frenetic urgency of a long-awaiting, bereaved beloved. They held each other's hands tightly in a way that their fingers were locked in an inextricable mess. They made love in the darkness of the cave. They merged into each other; they merged into the voluptuous body of the Earth, into the infinite stretches of the fathomless universe.

They merged into rivers and the hills and the mountains and the trees; they merged into the sporadic stir of leaves, into the messy entanglements of the boughs. They swam through the rivers, across the squashy ripples of their swelling waters; they glided across the widening stretches of the beaches; they mingled with the sonorous whisper of the branches, with the squeaky rustle of leaves of the darkening forests; they mingled with the giant body of the universe. They merged into the craters of the dead volcano, into the fire of the living volcano in its enormous rush towards the sky. They dipped into the sweetness of honey prepared by the bees, into the snake's venom paralyzing the prey in its diabolic, poison-fangs. They merged into the stubbornness of the rocks and also into the fickleness of the stream clung around its neck like a dazzling necklace.

They merged into the canines of the tiger and also into the extirpated flesh of its prey; they merged into the kaleidoscopic wings of the butterfly and also into the mucosal filth of the vermin.

A few night birds flew away over their heads with their dilated wings flapping tirelessly against the translucent, frigid evening air. The crimson light of the effulgent moon poured onto their wings like fire from heaven; they burst into wisps of incandescent flames. For a moment, Upananda and Kshema felt like being two night-birds with wings of fire flying into the uncharted depths of an ageless horizon. They traversed across the moon and the sun and the planets and the stars and the galaxies; they were celestial navigators now. They swung like pendulums across the freezing spaces of the universe. Its lurid, sweetness flew through their veins like a vascular stream; the fragrance of divinity emanating from their consecrated flesh spread through the mammoth profusion of space in an interminable universe like a sweet and succoring inebriation; they smelt the intoxicating sweetness of their blood in their noses, and were exhilarated by its primordial and atavistic effluvium. There was no obstacle there, no hindrance, no abounding and restrictive moral captivity; instead, there was an astronomic opulence of emptiness pouring on them, like the all-pervasive heaven's scrumptious and effusive blessing. They soared high up into the womb of the universe, into the depths of sprawling space where they no more heard the chantings "Buddham Saranam Gachhami" from the fecund Earth, neither did they have to follow there the Buddha's exasperating and abstemious Ten Commandments. They were liberated souls unchained from the shackles of the religion and its inviolable principles.

There was a heavenly delight in that togetherness. Theirs was a sojourn into the blissful arena of salvation. They felt every bit of it in those bracing moments of togetherness. They had perhaps achieved their salvation by now and for that they did not have to renounce their bodies; rather they achieved it through the consummation of their desire.

But after this abrupt episode of wakeful trance, Upananda and Kshema had by now come back to their senses.

An unknown bird on a tree's branches twittered for a moment and then, vanished into darkness.

"Where are we heading Upananda?" Kshema asked again.

Upananda pressed his face harder against her breasts and answered: "This uncertainty is the beauty of life. We will move where life drags us. How could you be so exhausted, Kshema?"

"But by relinquishing the path of salvation, have we not stepped into the dark, dungeon of sin, Upananda?"

After a moment's silence, Upananda answered: "The thing you consider as sin Kshema, is indeed great happiness. And salvation is also possible in that happiness."

In these moments of doubts, discussions and mutual adorations, their days were getting consumed happily. They no more felt the exhaustion of aimless wandering.

The other day, Upananda had gone deeper into the forest to collect fruits leaving Kshema near a large, leaf-crowded banyan tree. But when he returned, there was no Kshema there. Upananda was a little worried and he started searching for her in the vicinity. He called her in a loud voice: "Kshema! Kshema!" But there was no response. His loud voice ricocheted from the walls of the surrounding hills and returned in the form of multiple reverberations: "Kshema! . . . Kshema! . . . . Kshema! . . . . Kshema! . . . . . " The thundering echo of his voice startled the river and the hill and the forest with its thumping virulence and urgency. Upananda's desperation and energy knew no bounds and it seemed as if in one violent sweep of his hand he could tumble the whole forest into the river.

Upananda started running helter-skelter like a lunatic calling Kshema's name loudly time and again. Listening to his earsplitting voice, the deer grazing grass lifted their heads and stared at him—astounded and unblinking. A few pigeons hooting indiscriminately in the tangled boughs of some unknown tree, peeped at him, while the squirrels sliding across its branches paused for a moment, and gazed at him, with their tiny eyes glittering like pearls. A cobra hidden in an anthill lifted its hood and stared at the sprinting Upananda.

A sudden gush of unexpected rain along with a violent, wrecking whirlwind came from nowhere and blew Upananda's saffron dress away. His sinewy arms stiffened like granite rocks; his eyes glowed like a thousand irradiant suns. With a sense of reckless urgency, he looked around and saw a small waterfall on a hill, elongated like a silvery rope from the hilltop to the ground. Below the hill, there was a tiny reservoir on which the water fell making delicate and mellifluent rhythmic sounds. A fractured rainbow hung decorously in the air, formed by the sun's slanted rays fallen on the gushing water—streaming, gurgling and frothing. Upananda looked at the waterfall; Nature's shimmering affluence dilated his eyes in astonishment; he was dazed and overwhelmed. And then he heard a faint voice, piercing through the swollen, damp air like the exuberant and enrapturing humming of a bee. It was Kshema's voice. She sang a lullaby whose luring symphony spread all around like a delirious musical note.

Upananda recklessly darted in that direction and spotted Kshema bathing inside the waterfall. She was scantily dressed and the water falling on her body, in gushing streams, made her look winsomely elegant and provocative. Her long, black hair cascaded her uncovered back like a darkish, thinly-stripped curtain and her wetted thighs were tantalizingly visible. A few butterflies flapped their kaleidoscopic wings around her and created a twirling and shifting canvass of ebullient colours spiraling and gyrating in her vicinity like a gentle and exquisite whirlwind of colours. It looked as if bountiful Nature had imploded into Kshema's winding and curvaceous body to make her look more attractive, winsome and seductive. The curvy movements of her supple limbs maddened Upananda beyond his control. With an uncontrollably excited voice, he accosted her: "Kshema!"

Kshema looked back towards him with a mischievous and bashful smile and then started playing with the falling water, with a flirty and coquettish poise. Upananda rushed towards her while she feigned resistance and tried to escape, while secretly yearning that Upananda clasped her from behind, and possess her with a bullish, masterful potency. Upananda did the same and started kissing her, whimsically. Kshema enjoyed every moment of his impermissible flirtatiousness. Upananda lifted her soft, delicate body on his shoulder and frantically ran into the darkness of the cave.

This old cave was surrounded by the impenetrable and scrambled growth of the forest-grass. A few errant, whitish clouds hovered in the sky like dazzling, silvery saucers.

In the darkness of the cave, Upananda and Kshema opened up their bodies to each other. A wave of thrilling exhilaration cruised through their animated assemblage of nerves. The anonymous rush of madness traversing rapidly across their fired-up spines was scintillating, electrifying. It seemed as if their bodies were set ablaze, as if their arteries and nerves and tendons were on fire, primal, iridescent fire that set lusty, hungry bodies ablaze with the unrestricted overflow of carnality. The world between them had shrunk to nothingness; the tiny crammed space between them pullulated with the profligacy of their intrepid breaths.

After a few moments of exciting togetherness, Kshema pushed Upananda with her arms and ran into the long stretches of sand on the bank of river Sadanira. Upananda followed her like a possessed man.

Kshema lied quiet and denuded on the soft, spongy sand of Sadanira's bank spreading her voluptuous arms across the winding and curvy stretches of the river. For a moment, it seemed as if she was River Sadanira herself coursing before Upananda with its swift, sonorous flow. Upananda melted like ice into her enormous rush towards eternity. They glided through the ragged soil, through the depths of the forest, through the massive crowd of rocks caressing their mossy surfaces, through the empty ravines while drinking their lurid and hollowing emptiness to the lees. They flew through the intricate depths of the horizon, through the foggy cover of distant plateaus, through each other's throbbing veins, enmeshed like an inextricable loop.

Chapter V

After their ouster from 'Mahabana Vihara,' Upananda and Kshema however had not been able to digest this humiliation so easily with an air of cold and unfazed indifference.

They wandered aimlessly for a few days like dry leaves blown away by the wind; now they decided to make their humiliating ouster from the community an ethical issue. They roamed from region to region, from community to community and spread their story with proud and valiant hearts. It was the story of their rebellion, of their defiance, of their pugnacity against the religion's obstinate doggedness and dismal oppressiveness. It was the story of their conviction, of their resolute defection into another existence—that of freedom and licentiousness, of unbounded audacity to enjoy and relish the bounteous plenitude that a libertine and restriction-free life offered them. The younger disciples got fascinated and enamoured—with them, with their rebellious demeanour, with the tenacity of their resolve to confront the religion's doggedness and austerity. They listened to them with prodigious interest and enthusiasm.

Perhaps in a way, Upananda and Kshema represented the latter's own sexual cravings suppressed under the duplicitous garb of religion. Their audacity was their inspiration; their amorousness was their allurement; their violations were their encouragement. Upananda and Kshema became their consentient messiahs.

The women disciples thought that all the decorum

imposed on them was fabricated, artificial and illegitimate. They also wanted to revolt, but could not, due to the indelible weight of counterfeit morality thrust upon them by 'dharma.' But these impositions usually became counterproductive and led to unbounded moral and ethical infringements. The disciples roamed outside wearing the hallowed attire of religion; yet, they violated the commandments indiscriminately. Many of them encroached into the city-women's houses and developed illicit relationships with them when their husbands were away. They had become familiar names in the drinking and gambling houses of the city.

Disciple Bajrabahu's illicit romance with Baisali's businessman Suryakanta's daughter-in-law Chandrakanti was one burning instance.

Chandrakanti was married to the former's son Aryabira who, after their first night, went on a trading-voyage across the sea into far-off islands. But from that day onwards he was never seen again. Some of his fellow-voyagers from Baisali who returned home after a few years said that he had been captured and killed by sea-pirates. Some others said that he had started a new life with an unknown lady in a foreign island. Suryakanta, after prolonged and wearisome waiting for his son's return, finally accepted that he was dead and hence, completed all customary, religious death-rites for his son. Everybody had accepted that Aryabira was dead. Yet, Chandrakanti lived with a futile expectation that he will come back one day—an expectation that lingered in her psyche like the un-extinguished flame of a candle against the brute force of a ravaging storm.

A soft autumn afternoon! Disciple Bajrabahu came for begging in host Suryakanta's house where he was offered food, and after taking food, he was planning to move out before dusk. Chandrakanti accosted him through her chamber's window: "Bajrabahu!"

Bajrabahu felt the soft, quelling touch of her blushful voice deep within his soul. The sound of her bracelet and anklet rang in his ears like the sweet jingling symphony of some distant music. Her voice sounded soothing and enchanting like an enthralled cuckoo's tender, mellifluous singing from within a mango orchard's fog-enshrouded, dense foliage. It was like a tattler bird's musical twitter in the tranquil, moonlit sky.

Before Bajrabahu, appeared the pinkish-gown-clad, the golden-necklace-wearing, the fleshy-figured, the fair-complexioned, and the lustful Chandrakanti. An unprecedented swirl of sensuous naiveté emanated from the curvy movements of her agile body and penetrated deep into Bajrabahu's ravenous heart thereby igniting his subdued concupiscence into a flaming convulsion of desire. Bajrabahu heard her throbbing anklet's symphony deep within the dark and secret chambers of his prehensile heart. Hypnotized, he looked at Chandrakanti's gloomy and grief-stricken face; her eyes looked like two dazzling diamond pieces sparkling unhinderedly in the unexplored depths of a dark and inexplorable mine. She appeared before Bajrabahu like a lotus bloomed from Earth's incandescent viscera whose petals stretched right up to the furtive enclosures of his hideous heart. Bajrabahu was flabbergasted.

Nothing but the incessant flight of flocks of home-returning birds arching the skyline like a cosmic penumbra was visible in that indolent afternoon.

With the touch of Chandrakanti's deep breath on his skin, Bajrabahu got back to his senses. He looked uninterruptedly into the prolonging depths of her curvy body. Her face was almost washed by a few tear-drops fallen from her half-sunken eyes. Her softened lips looked like vibrating with a question.

Bajrabahu asked with a compassionate voice: "What would you ask me, dear?"

Chandrakanti stretched her left palm towards Bajrabahu and asked in a blushful voice: "Can you look at my palm and prognosticate whether my husband whom I had said adieu with the setting sun over River Ganga will return or not? He has left me after our first night and has never returned."

Bajrabahu held Chandrakanti's palm in his hands like a possessed man despite the fact that palm-telling was indeed a forbidden practice in their religion. Yet, he continued holding her palm in his hand in spite of the established and widely followed proscriptions. Through that infectious touch, he felt Chandrakanti's softness in his body, percolating through his craving torso like frenzied and magical whim. There was infinite contentment in that alluring touch, an instant realization of salvation in that momentary and infectious proximity. Bajrabahu told Chandrakanti in a gravelly tone: "Dear! Your husband shall return no more. Either he is killed by the sea-pirates or he has settled in a foreign land, having gotten married to an unknown lady." There were a few moments of silence that prevailed between Bajrabahu and Chandrakanti, except the faint twitter of home-returning birds from a distant and darkened horizon. Listening to the heart-breaking words from Bajrabahu, Chandrakanti left without uttering a single syllable, leaving nothing but a long-stretching void before the hypnotized Bajrabahu and nothing else.

Bajrabahu got back to his senses, but Chandrakanti had left by now. His wakeful trance had come to an end in the midst of the pigeons' relentless hooting inside the sty.

From that day onwards, Bajrabahu stealthily frequented into Chandrakanti's secluded chamber in the darkness of the night and made love to her on her velvet-cushioned cot in the blinding depths of legion sinful nights. The dim table lamp flickering intermittently in the chamber's torrential deluge of darkness was the only witness to their iniquitous proximity. Bajrabahu filled the lingering vacuum in Chandrakanti's forlorn body with his tempestuous breaths. Her desiccated body tormented by Aryabira's longstanding absence stormily sprung into a renewed life's blustering invigoration. Bajrabahu opened Chandrakanti up inside the chamber's profound darkness; he opened her up by her face and plunged into the immeasurable depths of her eyes; he unfastened her gaudy attire in darkness; he dived into the inviting depths of her flesh that pleasantly reeked of the cold smell of the universe. He stroked her hair with immaculate care and precision. He buried his face in the softness of her breasts.

In the middle of the night, they escaped into the jungle and made love in the darkness of the abandoned grooves. Their sweet moans and whispers were engulfed by the deep murmur of the river and the soughing susurrations of the dense and impervious forest. They drank the cool water of the streams and bathed in the freezing, honeyed breeze of the night. They vagrant moon peeped through the clouds like a celestial eavesdropper and disappeared through the preternatural silence of the night like a clandestine burglar. A few night birds flew away over their head and congealed imperceptibly into the inscrutable depths of the forest like clusters of darkened shadows. And here in Chandrakanti's arms, slept Bajrabahu—hypnotized and contented—inebriated with the lurid fragrance of Chandrakanti's breaths while feeling the pleasures of ageless salvation in his quenched soul. Oh! What pleasure was there in that sinful togetherness! What consummated realization of eternal salvation! He had never achieved that in the tireless chantings of the mantras.

*****

Now Upananda had turned into the messiah of Bajrabahu and the likes. He had become their liberator from the incarceration of 'dharma,' from the dark dungeon of compulsive 'self-abnegation.' Upananda and Kshema roamed from community to community spreading their messages of rebellion.

After roaming like this from places to places, they finally came back to Baisali.

Slowly, the religion had started attracting lots of younger people from Royalty and other high-class families. The reason, of course, was not spiritual, but societal. Conversion into Buddhism had innumerable benefits. Firstly, wearing the saffron attire itself commanded boundless public veneration and secondly, the blind-believing commoners could easily be exploited in the name of religion. For a disciple, the religion now offered a blissful life of unhindered wealth, plentitude and exuberance. More so, he could also receive lots of royal grants and amenities.

A disciple called Anathapindada had once gifted Buddha a luxury-garden named 'Jetabana.' The former had bought the garden for a gold coin per inch. Anathapindada had great devotion for Tathagata and had unflinching faith in his propagated religion. Now a royal person named Dhananjaya gifted Upananda his 'Ashokabana.' But it was a well-understood fact that he did it not for a spiritual reason, but for fame and social respectability that could now be easily earned by wealth. The community was held in high esteem in the public eye and was receiving bounteous royal patronage for its religious programs and activities. Dhananjaya knew the benefits and importance of being its sagacious promoter.

Dhananjaya's gifted garden had a huge, palatial mansion inside its premise. From this mansion, Upananda propagated his new 'dharma'—a 'dharma' of deviation and licentiousness. The garden came to be known as 'Ashokabana Vihara'—the ashram of Gurus Upananda and Kshema.

Every day, large contingents of disciples assembled in 'Ashokabana Vihara' to listen to Upananda's sermons. Upananda said: "Dear disciples! Consummation of desire is the pathway to salvation. Exploration of the body is not a sinful activity at all; rather, in bodily fulfillment, lie the realization of divinity and the prospect of salvation—your much-adored salvation. Explore your bodies disciples! Explore your bodies to the full. There is no salvation in the tedious and senseless recitation of mantras; it is right there in the plump body of your beloved reeking of the aroma of a deer's musk, in the sweet, bewitching fragrance of her torpid breaths lulling you to sleep in the fathomless depths of their eyes. It is right there in the in the whirling curvature of their bodies into whose ravishing depths you plunge like bees into honeycombs, like insects into engulfing pitcher plants." Upananda went on . . .

The disciples rose in ceremonial uproar. Upananda's newfangled method became their indubitable mantra for salvation. His method seemed to be convincing, enjoyable and scrumptious. They relished the licentious freedom it offered to them. There was ecstasy in that freedom; there was joy in that exploration; there was prompt realization of divinity in that quizzical, carnal venture. This new religion attracted them greatly; it was the religion of blood, of instinct, of desire, of flesh and it was amenable to many. For Upananda, it was the panacea for all grief and suffering.

Upananda's preachings were diametrically averse to Lord Buddha's. Yet he had firm conviction in his newfangled and newly propagated thought and philosophy. He had no qualm, no, inhibition and no compunction in taking easy recourse to the forbidden and transgressive path of licentiousness. He thought Lord Buddha wasted his life in running after a mirage, a meaningless vacuum that he foolishly called salvation. Salvation was right there in his father's kingdom of Kapilabastu, in the brimming effervescence of liquor frothing bubbly and bouncily inside crystal-clear glasses, in the delicate symphony of the anklets of city-whores dancing drunkenly in the dim light of the palace's glittering chandeliers. Salvation was right there in their smooth, subtle and aromatic bodies with which he could have slept on the royal palace's velvety-cushioned, ivory-cots. Salvation was there in the mirthful exploration of the nudity of their bodies in the tranquility of moon-blanched nights.

Upananda's argument was sharp like a knife's edge. While delivering sermons to the disciples in 'Ashokabana Vihara,' he said: "Tathagata had said everything is untrue and illusory. If that is the case, then why would a pinch of salt in food be a monstrous obstacle to the attainment of salvation? Is that pinch of salt not an illusion? In that case, what is the harm in mixing it with food and then eating it?"

The congregated disciples hailed his arguments with loud and ceremonial applause. Some of them snorted: "Who would eat that tasteless food in the host's house every day?"

Upananda continued: "If the salt-less food did not have any attraction, then why did the older gurus run from house to house for it in the scorching heat of the conflagrant sun?"

Nobody had an answer to this question.

However, there were some who raised eyebrows. A disciple asked: "But eating meat is strictly prohibited for disciples. And these days, they are found eating meat in the hosts' houses."

Upananda answered with a gentle smile: "Don't you know that Tathagata while on his way to Kushinagar, fell ill after eating pork in a potter's house and died. Then why should there be an obstruction to eating meat? Even Tathagata did not detest it."

But the disciple argued: "As per our conventions, there is no harm in eating the meat of an animal that had been killed inadvertently. But killing an animal knowingly and eating its meat is unpardonable sin."

Upananda answered with another smile: "But how can you kill an animal unknowingly? The principle you are talking about is nothing but a sham, a treachery. What is the difference between eating meat knowingly and doing the same unknowingly?"

Yes, a similar incident did happen. Four disciples ventured into a host's house for food at Baisali's outskirts. After reaching there, they spotted a female deer roaming with her offspring inside an adjacent garden. They readily expressed their desire to eat the latter's meat while the host hesitated to kill the little deer. But the disciples threatened him with a curse and in fear, he killed the deer's offspring and offered its meat to them, that too beyond noon.

The disciples were convinced that such violations were harmless and acceptable. One of them said: "If Tathagata could achieve salvation after eating pork, then why should we be prohibited from eating meat?" The disciples hailed Upananda with thunderous claps. Their echoes and reverberations were heard in distant mountains and ravines. Disturbed by the sound of the huge and uproarious claps, a flock of cranes congealed into the leafy branches of a tree suddenly flew into the sky and hung in the air like bright, silvery medallions.

'Ashokabana Vihara' became the centre of these new learnings and was filled with countless numbers of disciples. Upananda and Kshema became their gurus, their messiahs, their saviours. The number of younger male and female disciples in the Vihara started multiplying exponentially. They believed that salvation could be achieved through Guru Upananda's prescribed method only.

When the older gurus came to know about these developments, they put fingers into their ears. They could see that a catastrophe was emerging like a curse from heaven and was going to devour their holy and celebrated religion like the devilish 'Rahu'[19] engulfing the bright moon in a dark-moon night. They knew that a terrible disaster was in the offing. They also knew that the blasphemous Upananda will be its initiator, its promoter and its facilitator. They could see that a diabolic evil force that was going to sweep across their holy and sanctified 'dharma' like a blight, like an anathema. They prayed to Tathagata with folded hands: "Save us Lord! Save us. The darkness of evil is going to engulf us all. Save us holy Buddha. Save us."

They also roamed from community to community calling Upananda a gruesome violator of 'dharma.'

But what the common people could have done about it? They did not have much comprehension of the finer principles of 'dharma' and thus, did not understand the intricacy of the matter. They brushed it aside calling it a temporary internal conflict between the two divided and ideologically conflicted groups of the community.

■

---

[19]   In Hindu mythology, it is an evil spirit that engulfs the moon in a dark-moon night because of which the denizens of Earth are not able to see the moon for quite some time.

Chapter VI

The calm and tranquil 'Mahabana Vihara' of Baisali!

The afternoon had faded while giving way, willfully, to the approaching evening. The sun had descended across the distant horizon like an extinguished fireball.

Usually by this time, the air in 'Mahabana Vihara' reverberated with chantings of mantras and recitations of sermons. But now, one heard them only from a few, secluded chambers; and the other rooms with stone-beds mostly lay empty and abandoned. The disciples were busy eating delicious meal in the hosts' houses, even after 'noon.' Some of them roamed on the streets of Baisali rejoicing, merry-making. Some also loitered in front of city women's houses with the hope that some of them might allow them to get in. The reason was that they knew palmistry.

Kashyapa rubbed his forehead, emitted a deep and prolonged sigh of helplessness and said in a destitute voice: "Lord Tathagata! Save us from blasphemy. Save us from blasphemy."

Before him, was splayed a Buddhist scripture, in a state of utter dereliction on a worn-out, dilapidated mat, with its yellowed, wasp-infested, palm-leaf-pages left wide open. He sat mum in his room.

Guru Kubjasobhita had also started noticing similar, rampant violations in Pataliputra.

Kubjasobhita said in a trembling voice: "Dear Kashyapa! I think we should immediately draw 'Dharmashoka's attention towards such horrid, superabundant transgressions by these detestable herds of aberrant younger disciples. He is now our religion's chief patron and promoter."

Kashyapa, Yasha and Upali shrieked together with expressive gestures of utter stupefaction as if they had fallen from the sky; they asked conjointly in a dumbfounded voice: "Who is this 'Dharmashoka'?"

Kubjasobhita answered: "After the *Kalinga War*, Chandashoka has turned into Dharmashoka. Don't you all know that? He has erected multiple rock edicts at different sacred places and has declared himself "Debanang Priyadarshi" (the favourite of gods). He is Bodhisattva who has descended to Earth to protect 'dharma.' Don't you know all these?"

Yasha asked: "O God! When did this Chandashoka become Dharmashoka? This cruel and savage mass murderer! Don't you all know how as his father Magadha king Bindusara's lieutenant, he eliminated rebelling citizens like extinguishing a spark of fire by trampling it under one's feet? Don't you know how he had turned Takshasila's holy and pietistic soil red with mass murder and bloodshed? Don't you know how savagely and maliciously he had slaughtered his elder brother Bitashoka—Magadha's real and legitimate heir-apparent —to occupy the throne?"

There was a notable expression of contempt and disgust in Yasha's voice.

Upali said; "This is really strange. How could this bloodthirsty Chandashoka become Dharmashoka overnight? This ruthless slaughterer of ninety-nine brothers!"

Chandashoka's coronation was delayed by four years for this reason. In these four years, he had not only slaughtered the ninety-nine brothers, but also had wiped out their supporters and accomplices from the face of Earth, in a massive and internecine pogrom that perhaps would find no matching equivalence in History. In his kitchen, everyday hundreds of animals were slaughtered for the preparation of soup. He was truly Kalashoka, aptly justifying the inherent heinousness of his name. But the astounding fact that he had now transformed himself into Dharmashoka was beyond Upali's honest comprehension. This mindboggling transformation, for Upali, was nothing but a mockery of 'dharma,' a travesty of generosity and, a caricature of rectitude.

Upali continued: "But what is the need for a king in the Buddhist community? Tathagata himself had relinquished his throne to become a monk. But this king rules under the ostentatious garb of religion. Is it not an illusion and a pretension? It's all possible for a hypocritical monarch like him."

Kubjasobhita answered: "They say that Ashoka repented heavily after the War. But it was not really a war; it was a heartless pogrom inflicted on an innocent race of peasants, and blacksmiths and traders and priests . . . Kalinga had so far been an undefeated feudal territory and its denizens were known for their wealth and prosperity in agriculture and trade; their tradesmen travel to distant, beyond sea islands like Java and Sumatra for trade and commerce. Starting from Maurya Chandragupta till Bindusara, nobody had dared to vanquish this independent state that flourished with peace, stability and economic prosperity. But in the twelfth year of his rule, Ashoka took a heinous vow to occupy this yet unconquered Kalinga but for which his thirst for territorial expansion would not have been quenched."

Kubjasobhita continued: "One day, Ashoka's bloodthirsty army attacked Kalinga. They slaughtered its feudal lords along with their soldiers, their commoners, their peasants, their priests, their women, their children . . . The waters of rivers like Daya and Kushabhadra turned red with the blood of the slain Kalingas spilled onto their holy water surfaces. The sky trembled with the screams of their ravished women. Ashoka's soldiers burnt everything into ashes . . . habitations, cornfields . . . everything. Virgins were ravished. Children were thrown into fire. The old and the infirm were also not spared. Their heads were chopped off and thrown on the streets. Those who survived were imprisoned and brought to Pataliputra as slaves."

Kubjasobhita continued: "River Daya's bank was filled

with corpses. Severed heads, chopped off limbs, strewn intestines all around . . . It was a ghastly scene. River Daya had turned into an eerie and dreadful pool of blood. The empty horizon was filled with screams, with laughters, with cries . . . And then came the Kalinga women, in throngs and clusters, in the ferocious depths of dark nights, and madly scrambled for their slain husbands' bodies from amidst the ghastly mound of lacerated corpses. The feeble lamps in their hands glittered peevishly amidst brooding darkness, yet they couldn't find the bodies of their loved ones. They beat their chests insanely and cried vociferously through the blinding depths of the cruel and insouciant nights. But all in vain! Their cries were heartrending; they pierced through the night's dark heart, like invisible arrows. History bled with their screams.

Tigers came prowling from nearby jungles, dragged away bodies into the forests, ate them up. Jackals ran helter-skelter with chopped off limbs in their mouths. Blood dripped from their mouths like raindrops. Vultures came flying from unknown horizons, plunged onto the bodies and drank their blood. Wild dogs came rushing from nowhere and picked the bones in their salivating mouths and vanished. And then came the ransacking army of worms from the underground, and pounced on the corpses, got into them, ate them up, cleaned them up . . .

Chandashoka stood on Dhauli-Hill with his blood-stained dagger in his hand, and laughed, and laughed boisterously. There was mockery in that laughter, at the sky and its deep profusion of emptiness, at the gods and their appalling helplessness. He was now the undisputed monarch of Aryabarta."

Kubjasobhita paused for a moment after this prolonged and impassioned description of the war and said: "In the world history, Chandashoka's capture of Kalinga is nothing but a mass pogrom in the name of war. After his victory over Kalinga, Ashoka had hardly any territory left to occupy in Aryabarta except a few smaller ones in the South."

Yasha said: "But I think Chandashoka's conversion to Buddhism is nothing but his strategy to safeguard his bloodily constructed empire. It's no more than a political gimmick."

Upali also doubted the same and said: "Cunning people only know such tricks."

Kubjasobhita asked: "If a killer like dacoit Angulimala could be converted into a Buddhist monk by Tathagata, then why can Chandashoka not become Dharmashoka?"

"Dacoit Angulimala and Chandashoka possess a similar character. But how can a monarch ever be a begging disciple? Can a scepter, a blood-stained dagger and a begging bowl stay together? Angulimala's case was different. He was a dacoit who got himself transformed into a saint. But Chandashoka is still the monarch. His so-called transformation is nothing but a bare-faced lie, a repugnant sham." Yasha argued.

Dacoit Ratnakar could become Valmiki. But how could the monarch become a saint? He could not imagine.

Upali told: "But History is replete with such instances where the kings have baffled people like this, all the time. They have projected themselves as their messiahs by taking easy recourse to religion. Chandashoka is doing the same. But is he solely responsible for this? Who inducted him into the religion? Who brought this thug into the holy religion of ours?"

Kubjasobhita briefly answered: "It is none other than Pataliputra's Upagupta."

Hearing Upagupta's name, Yasha screamed: "O! Upagupta! That deviant guru! Gurus like him can only transform a Chandashoka into Dharmashoka. They do it for royal patronage and reinforcement. They can sacrifice the religion for selfish purposes. Do you know that this Upagupta was once thrown out of the community for his irremediably transgressive and deviant behavior?"

Yasha continued: "Upagupta had mastered hypnotism and illusionism using which he could earn plenty of money from businessmen and royal personages. After being dispelled from the community, he was gifted with a magnificent and palatial mansion by a rich man from this city, where he lives with a young disciple who serves him with profound devotion and veneration. But do you know that this boy, before becoming a disciple, has not even received prior permission from his parents, which is an indispensable prerequisite according to Buddhist law? Possibly, Upagupta has cunningly hypnotized that boy to become a disciple. We must not forget that even Tathagata, before admitting his son Rahul into the community, had solicited permission from his father and Rahul's grandfather, king Suddhodana. It's on the latter's request that it was made an uninfringeable and sacrosanct law in our religion that anybody who becomes a disciple must first of all obtain prior permission from their parents without which their entry into religion was officiously countermanded. The child now may attain salvation. But what is the worth of achieving it at the cost of his parents' happiness? But this Upagupta is heedless of such laws and principles; he only knows to fulfill his personal interest and ambition. So I am not surprised he has turned Chandashoka into Dharmashoka, by dint of his own religious patronage, volitionally. A fraudulent guru like him is capable of indulging in such nefarious maneuvers without even an iota of moral and ethical compunction . . . A monarch can never be a disciple. You rest assured that the community's complete annihilation is at hand."

Kubjasobhita responded in a trembling voice: "When Chandashoka has already turned into Dharmashoka, we should rather use his patronage for the protection of our religion. That would be a prudent act of foresight. Otherwise, who would listen to a few decrepit and marginalized hundred-year old gurus like us? Raising your voice against someone like Chandashoka would be like throwing stones at a mountain."

Yasha responded in a doubtful voice: "Your proposal is most welcome. But why would Chandashoka listen to older gurus like us instead of listening to the younger ones who have already succumbed to licentious ways of life, willfully and who would not hesitate to glorify him for the sake of cheap material favours? What benefit he or his empire would get out of clinging to feckless bunches of old and infirm gurus like us?"

Kubjasobhita answered: "What is the harm in trying once? Dharmashoka has already made multiple announcements in different rock edicts for the protection of our religion."

The discussion ended there. It was finally decided that Kubjasobhita shall go to Pataliputra in the guise of an informal courtesy-visit and request Dharmashoka to offer royal patronage to the large Buddhist congregation that they were going to arrange. Such a congregation would never be possible without his royal patronage and reinforcement extended to them by him. Kubjasobhita was entrusted with the responsibility to try to convince the monarch that the recent deviations and violations happening to the religion by these younger, freaky and aberrant disciples are not for its good. It has to stop and the principle-abiding older gurus must be given command. After that, everything will be left to Tathagata.

Kashyapa felt assured a bit.

Chapter VII

Monarch Ashoka's capital city of Pataliputra! It was no more the remote and unknown Pataligrama of Ajatasatru's Magadha. Now it was the heart and soul of the dynasty, of the whole Aryan landscape!

It was 'Dharmashoka's royal conference hall.

The monarch's golden throne blazed like a smoldering star; it had four golden legs constructed in the shape of hungry lions; their polished-marble-made canines glowed like the ghastly image of death hovering right in front the congregated, aghast courtiers. From the marble ceiling above, hanged huge, gigantic chandeliers made of diamond and gemstones. They reflected and refracted the sun rays in the day and the moonbeams in the night; it created in the hall a rich, kaleidoscopic fiesta of colours. The gemstones, designedly planted at the top of the throne, created an illusion of a burning halo hanging decorously over the monarch's head, like an astral object. His golden crown was embellished with rare gems that mocked even the shining stars and galaxies in the sky lying scattered on its outstretched vault like mere, gleaming trinkets and gimcracks. It seemed as if the immeasurable, zillion splendors of the universe had imploded into the tiny, little globular space of monarch Ashoka's crown.

On the court's walls, were stuck gigantic graffiti of the monarch's glorious ancestors like Chandragupta Maurya, Bindusara etc. They flaunted their armoured chests with a humongous display of pride and valour while holding dazzling, sharp-edged swords in their hands. Even their dead eyes sparkled with valiance and grandeur.

Below every lion's foot, was placed a symbolic wheel representing 'dharma.' Every wheel was caught like a hapless deer in the lion's sharp, predatory claw that knew only to kill. The lions represented Dharmashoka's wolfish, bestial powers.

The architectural design of Dharmashoka's throne was also emblematic of his savage, brutality. It exposed his bestiality even though he might have wanted to camouflage it beneath the raiment of his flashy and grandiose entry into fraudulent religiosity.

Dharmashoka's head was tonsured like that of a Buddhist monk.

But his tonsured head made him look even more cruel, malicious and savage. Even his saintly saffron attire could not camouflage his archetypal viciousness. Rather, his savage truculence looked more glaring, prominent and dashing from within the masking veil of this artificial and ill-fitted countenance.

At the back of the throne were standing a group of Bhima-like bodyguards, garrisoned in a half-circle, holding sharp and glistening weapons in their hands. After getting transformed into Dharmashoka, even though superficially, the monarch relentlessly feared for his life. His past crimes including the deceptive and coldblooded murder of his brothers and other royal personages followed him like harrowing, surreptitious ghosts and kept haunting him in the depths of serene and assuaging nights. He usually did not have good sleep in the night due to a constant and nagging threat perception to his life. That is why he was always surrounded by his bodyguards starting from his royal durbar to his bedroom, day and night. But some people kept whispering amongst themselves that it was nothing but the paranoid behaviour of a bloodthirsty lunatic.

Behind the soldiers were standing beautiful maidens holding flower-bouquets in their hands. They used to throw flowers onto monarch Ashoka, at regular and periodic intervals, during the royal court's proceedings. These maidens were voluptuously dressed with the attractive parts of their plump bodies inadequately covered.

Many of them were in fact monarch Ashoka's concubines. Every other night, one of them slept with him to gratify his unquenchable thirst. Every night he entered into her throbbing body like a carnivorous beast, chewed morsels of her flesh with his sharp, protruding canines, injected his bestiality into the boundless depths of her immured soul, extirpated her body into scattered lumps of opened-up flesh and then, left her for another night. Her screams vanished in the darkness like an enigma and was engraved inside the stone walls like a hushed-up mystery. Her ravished body fluttered inside the monarch's clenched teeth like a frog fluttering inside a venomous snake's poison-fangs. She was then ready for another night, to die another death, to be devoured by its abysmal reservoir of sin, of filth, of unbridled savagery.

Monarch Ashoka's execution chamber (known as Ashoka's Hell) was situated inside a garden. It was an exquisitely beautiful garden filled with attractive, flowering trees, a swiftly flowing stream, and a crystal-clear lake overflowing with undulating, pellucid waters. Above the garden floated the limitless firmament of the sky and at a distance, ran the prolonging and gorgeous ravines of the surrounding mountains. The scenic beauty of the place was eye-catching, appalling. On the foothills of the mountains, the female peacocks enjoyed the dance of their male counterparts and kissed them through their beaks in an ecstasy of love and mutual adoration. In the nearby grassland, innumerable rams roamed with unbounded joy and exaltation. At a distance, female deer looked at their own reflections in a pond's crystal-clear water and were lost in the secret appreciation of their own beauty.

The execution chamber was in fact a huge palatial building implanted with a splendid architectural design on its white-coloured body. On its whitewashed walls were adroitly carved sculptures of beautiful maidens and their male counterparts making love. A wholehearted celebration of carnality flashed profusely through their stone-carved eyes. The overall atmosphere surrounding the palace was that of joy, of celebration, of berserk amusement.

But inside the palace, there was nothing but the terrorizing reign of death. There were dazzling skeletons of executed people dangling from wooden racks. There were skulls placed in lines on the rock-made shelves. The dry wind passing through their holes reverberated with empty susurrations of death. On the rocky wall of the chamber, was dangling the graffiti of Yama[20] riding a gigantic black bull with sharp, coiling and ferocious horns. There was a terrifying expression of hideous ferocity in his dilated eyes; the colossal mace that he held in his hand made him look even more ghastly and baleful. In darkness, death spread its nebulous wings like a vulture inside the chamber and its lethal whisper through the immeasurable depths of the night shook even the skeletons with the tremors of an insidious terror.

Monarch Ashoka's chief executioner Girika was in command of the chamber. Girika looked like a monster. He was tall, muscular, had a long, sprawling moustache below his nose that ran around that area like a poisonous, black-coloured snake. He wore nothing above his waist and was thoroughly bare-bodied though a few crisscrossing gold necklaces (which he received from monarch Ashoka as gifts for his tremendous and unmatchable slaughtering credentials). His eyes were blood-red as he was perpetually under the heady spell of liquor. He held in his hand a large, double-edged sword that could cleave the body of a prisoner in one single, monstrous blow. Girika killed people without mercy and his orders were inviolable for his attendants.

Prisoners were killed in various ways inside the execution chamber. Some were beheaded by Girika and his attendants; some were stabbed on their bellies; their intestines were

---

[20] The god of death in Hindu mythology.

brought out and hanged on the walls. Some were thrown into large, iron-made cauldrons containing boiling oil inside.

That day, Monarch Ashoka visited the chamber and saw a bunch of people tied in chains and standing before Girika with terror-stricken, pitiful eyes. Looking at the monarch, Girika saluted him promptly. Monarch Ashoka asked: "Who are these filthy, abominable people, Girika?"

Girika answered: "My Lord! These are a bunch of people from Kalinga and they were spreading the information amongst the public that your conversion to Buddhism is nothing but a sham, an ostentatious lie told to the world. Our soldiers have captured them and brought them here to be punished once your highness pronounces his verdict. What shall be their punishment, my Lord?"

Monarch Ashoka looked at the innocent, hapless bunch of Kalingas with his cruel eyeballs rotating inside their sockets like a pair of hellish, conflagrant fireballs that could burn everything to ashes with their continual and profusive emission of burning rays. And then with a thunderous voice, he shouted: "Throw them into the cauldron."

The Kalinga prisoners were immediately thrown into the cauldron containing boiling oil. They boiled like fishes; their disintegrating flesh melted and mingled into the thick, viscous oil like melted tar. They screeched and screamed. Their screeches filled the chamber with their undulating vibrations and the boiling cauldron's malodorous smoke filled the chamber like an abominable curse from Hell. Looking at the fluttering bodies of the Kalingas, monarch Ashoka started laughing loudly—a laughter that spread through the caliginous air of the chamber with thumping resonances and devoured those screams and screeches within moments.

In the meanwhile, his attendant Daruna came inside and bowed before him with drooped shoulders.

Monarch Ashoka asked: "Tell me Daruna! What news you have brought?"

Daruna told with a downcast head: "My Lord! Lots of Buddhist gurus have come to meet you."

Monarch Ashoka nodded and hastily went out of the chamber.

Much before, he had received prior information about the advent of lots of elderly Buddhist gurus from long distances to meet him, presumably to receive his royal patronage for the forthcoming mega-Buddhist conference. But since he was engaged in prolonged discussions with other religious leaders from Anga, Kalinga, Srabasti and Abanti etc., the Buddhist gurus had to wait for a long time. They started feeling exhausted.

That day Kalinga's religious guru Tishya was present there.

Tishya was Ashoka's youngest brother. He wore elegant saffron attire; his head was tonsured; he held a begging bowl in his hand and could act adroitly like a Buddhist guru. There was unmatchable grace and honour in his fabricated and refined demeanour. After the War, Ashoka had appointed him as Kalinga's religious guru, not so much for the propagation of 'dharma,' but to closely monitor even the remotest possibility of insurgency in the war-devastated Kalinga. Chandashoka had turned Kalinga into a massive crematorium filled with human skulls and skeletons and bones; but he was afraid of the new, resurgent lives that might have sprouted in them, after prolonged years of hibernation and sterility. That is why whatever territory he won, he appointed there a cunning lieutenant of his own in the guise of a saffron-attire-clad Buddhist monk so that he remained informed even of the slightest stir of insurgency in Kalinga. All the religious gurus like Tishya were amongst Ashoka's kith and kin and lieutenants.

They had already confided to Ashoka that things were under absolute control in his conquered territories and there is no imminent possibility of rebellion, even by the wildest stretch of imagination. They had nothing more to say.

At last, Tishya said: "My Lord! Kalinga has, now turned

thoroughly calm, defenseless, and peaceful. They have lost all their vestigial strength to even utter a single word against the mighty and the immensely powerful kingdom of Magadha. The utterance of its very name terrifies them, and sends rippling waves of mortifying terror across their quivering clusters of dry, withered bones. I have clandestinely employed there our secret informers in the guise of dedicated Buddhist disciples to spread the message of spirituality amongst the innocent public who are completely uninformed and oblivious of our intricate, strategic maneuvers. They will convince people that Dharmashoka is their ultimate and inevitable savior; he is Bodhisattva—Lord Buddha's holy reincarnation—who has descended onto Earth to be their benevolent and sagacious savior and rescuer. So there is no question of any kind of threat that the war-devastated and thoroughly annihilated Kalinga can pose to our ever-victorious kingdom of Magadha. In the meanwhile, I have erected a few rock edicts in places like Khandagiri, Udaygiri, Dhauligiri and Ratnagiri in Kalinga, as immensely visible insignias of your phenomenal and redeeming transformation from 'Kalashoka' to 'Dharmashoka,' of your majestic entry into the sanctified terrains of religious virtuosity. On every rock-edict, your name is inscribed as the ultimate saviour of mankind."

Monarch Dharmashoka emitted a faint, wry smile that, of course, did elicit a clandestine and sinister note of sarcasm and devilish contentment. He was happily assured that Kalinga is no more a threat to Magadha's celebrated and uncontested sovereignty.

He asked: "But Tishya! Do the Kalinga's citizens believe your words?"

Tishya answered: "You know great king that they are a bunch of innocent and harmless people. They foolishly believe that after witnessing the devastations of the war, you are burning in the purgatory fire of repentance and every moment, the traumatic memory of the war inflicted on Kalinga by you pricks your conscience like a nagging and excruciating sting of pain. They also think that you have thoroughly relinquished your characteristic and archetypal heinousness and have become transformed into an entirely religious person."

At this, Monarch Ashoka started laughing vociferously; Tishya joined him like a slavish follower. Their laughter splayed on the floor like the dazzling splinters of a broken glass; their ferocious rhythm and jingling cadence filled the chamber with their noxious echoes and reverberations; it seemed for a moment as if that hellish, infernal chamber was filled with death's cruel and intimidating laughter from Hell. The laughter stopped after a long time.

And then monarch Ashoka suddenly became serious eliciting a note of enduring and religious steadfastness on his face and said: "I have decided that now we shall start a religious movement from Magadha on a much larger scale and dimension. Once people get progressively involved in this movement, they would no more think of war. We shall be safe and secure forever inside our territory guarded by the protective walls of religion."

"What is this religious movement, my lord?" Asked Magadha's religious guru Dharmadutta Mogalayana.

Dharmashoka answered in a composed voice: "Before our times, the kings and monarchs used to initiate movements of war or hunting expeditions; but now we will start movements of 'dharma.' And with us, there will be disciples reciting lines from holy scriptures, roaming from community to community, from habitation to habitation spreading amongst the common populace the spiritual messages of Lord Buddha. Every citizen shall be compulsively converted into a Buddhist disciple. They will be turned into holy and astute pursuers of salvation, rather than being allowed to remain as punitive and spiteful contemplators of revenge and war."

Listening to this, the gurus accumulated in the chamber hailed him loudly by saying: "Great! Great!"

After these gurus left, the Buddhist disciples sitting in the room recited:

"Buddham saranam gacchami,

Dharmam saranam gacchami

Sangham saranam gacchami"

These recitations heavily sanctified the inner space of the closed compartment.

In the meanwhile, came into the room Kubjasobhita— weak, old and bent at the waist. He was followed by gurus like Kashyapa, Yasha, Upali and a few others.

They shouted in a collective voice: "Long live monarch Ashoka. Long live the monarch."

Dharmashoka welcomed them with folded hands.

After that, Yasha said: "Dharmashoka! Our religion is under serious threat today and is on the verge of possible extinction from the face of Earth. You are its saviour. If in today's troubled times you do not protect the religion, then it will disappear within no time from this Jambu island."

Monarch Ashoka had already received prior information regarding the lately burgeoning indiscipline in the religion. He also knew that this decrepit bunch of older gurus had become irrelevant and marginalized inside their own community and have become a minority relegated to the peripheral realms of insignificance and inactivity. Of course, it must be understood that their desertion was due to their uncompromisingly strict and disciplinarian attitude, which even Lord Buddha had not stringently advocated. He had never been a dauntless advocator of too much of discipline in the observation of 'dharma' and was fairly moderate in the dissemination of his principles which were modestly liberal and reasonably sustainable. It was true that he had propagated the religion; but he was never a strict and ruthless disciplinarian as a prophet. But the older gurus made the rules too harsh and obtrusive which counterproductively led to their own desecration.

The older gurus went on eulogizing the monarch profusely; but the latter, with all his inherent cunningness, only knew that it was nothing but an outward show, an ostentatious facade.

But he did not want to disappoint them either. Rather he thought to keep them in hand, for the time being, for his own political benefit.

Monarch Ashoka assured them with a full-throated voice and said: "Sure! Sure! You all are respected gurus of the religion. To extend all kinds of help and assistance to you is my prime obligation as a perspicacious protector of 'dharma.'"

Then he ordered the treasurer: "Give one thousand gold coins to the gurus."

"But what is their use for us? According to Buddhist principles, we are prohibited to even touch gold. It is sinful and a sacrilegious." The gurus screamed in a collective voice.

Monarch Ashoka looked at them in a clandestinely snobbish and condescending gesture and emitted a wry smile. "How stupid these monks are? They have not yet understood the value of gold." He told himself.

Kashyapa told: "Dharmashoka! A handful of rice before sunset in the hosts' house is more than adequate for us. The saffron dress that we are offered by them during the winter is good enough for us to cover our bodies. The little coins that we are gifted by the hosts are more than sufficient for us to run the community. If being driven by gluttony we accept more than that what we need, then it will be tantamount to a heretical deviation in our 'dharma' and a sacrilegious transgression of our obligatory principles of ethics and morality. We want your munificent patronage only for the sake of the large and redeeming Buddhist conference that we are going to arrange to rescue our religion from thoroughgoing desecration in the hands of this ignominious bunch of deviant disciples."

A faint, pompous ray of smile flickered on Dharmashoka's lips. But, of course, it was always riddled with a surreptitious note of sarcasm.

"These are a bunch of stupid, imbecilic and senseless people. They won't understand the worth of gold." Dharmashoka told himself and continued: "You don't worry. Pataliputra shall shoulder the responsibility of all the essential arrangements, and shall extend every kind of logistic and financial assistance that you require and all your requisitions shall be readily complied with. You rest assured. Buddhism shall indefatigably continue to prevail as the dominant religion in my kingdom."

The older gurus felt tremendously reassured with monarch Ashoka's kind and confidence-providing words of pledge and reaffirmation.

After they left, there came into Dharmashoka's durbar hundreds of younger disciples chanting the words: "Glory to Dharmashoka! Glory to Dharmashoka!" They spread out in the inner space of the monarch's chamber like pullulating clusters of lilies spreading across the rippling and undulatory surface of a large pond filled with darkish, pellucid water. Dharmashoka's eyes flew over that pond like two humming and buzzing black bees gyrating incessantly around its elliptical circumference.

The younger disciples were being led by Upananda and Kshema of Baisali's 'Ashokabana Vihara.' They shouted: "Glory to Dharmashoka."

The accompanying disciples shouted along with them: "Glory to Dharmashoka."

Dharmashoka responded with a smiling face: "We welcome you all."

Upananda said in an appeasing voice: "My lord! You are the great Dharmashoka—the unblemished protector of 'dharma.' We have come here with great hope and expectation to receive your royal patronage."

In response, Pataliputra's religious guru said: "The protection of 'dharma' is now Dharmashoka's sole and scared responsibility. He has constructed such a huge, expansive empire only with the holy and dedicated purpose of the religion's extensive and global promulgation. You all are sufficiently aware of his congenital disinterestedness in power and ascendency. His only interest now lies in the planetary propagation of 'dharma.'"

Dharmashoka lifted his gracious and benevolent hand in a gesture of generous reassurance and said: "I need religiously committed disciples like you for the propagation of 'dharma' not only in my kingdom but also in states on Bharata's west like Kabul, Kandahar and Hirat. I shall send prince Mahendra to the southern state of Singhala."

Pataliputra's religious guru added: "What Lord Tathagata himself could not achieve for the religion despite his whole lifetime's sacrifice shall now be accomplished by monarch Ashoka with a mere blink of the eye. You stay assured."

The younger disciples shouted: "Glory to monarch Ashoka! Glory to monarch Ashoka."

Monarch Ashoka knew that these younger disciples are the ones who would propagate 'dharma' on his behalf; and gradually, his notorious Kalashoka image shall be permanently obliterated from peoples' ever-forgetful mind. It would readily transform his blackened and disingenuous image of 'Kalashoka' into that of an essentially spiritual and compassionate 'Dharmashoka.' The older gurus would be grossly unfit for this job.

Upananda said complainingly: "But O Lord! We are mercilessly thrown into the midst of a dire and helpless situation today; we are left embroiled in an inescapable quagmire. The older gurus proclaim themselves as the lone custodians of 'dharma': they have incarcerated us in stringent and obligatory rules and regulations and have hijacked the religion into their unchallengeable command and control. In the name of discipline, they remorselessly disown us from the community for very small and negligible mistakes. In this situation, we feel horribly insecure and if you don't patronize us, then we will be thoroughly demoralized, broken-hearted."

Dharmashoka assured them from the throne by saying: "In my understanding, the days of the hundred-year-old gurus are long gone. How can they protect the religion of such widespread expansiveness with their skins slackened and their teeth fallen? For the protection of 'dharma,' we need younger, and exuberant people like you who are full of undaunted spirit and vivacity."

Upananda said: "The older gurus have empowered a hundred-fifty-year-old Rebata to take the final call on our permanent ouster from the community, my Lord."

Dharmashoka told: "You stay assured. They had come and approached me a little while ago soliciting my royal patronage in the forthcoming mega-conference. I am giving you assurance that you will emerge victorious in that unique and auspicious event. Our gurus shall shoulder the responsibility of bringing together hundreds and hundreds of younger disciples from across the kingdom, and also from places lying beyond our territorial boundary to participate in the conference. The older ones are completely unaware of the magnitude and seriousness of your preparation to demolish them in that event, and their placid complacency will be their biggest flaw. In the least, you can easily beat them on the basis of your sheer number."

The younger disciples shouted in a large and congregated voice: "Glory to Dharmashoka."

After the shouting subsided, monarch Dharmashoka called his treasurer and ordered: "Give these people one thousand gold coins. They will prepare for the mega conference."

Upananda and his followers went back elated.

Then there were seen large congregations of younger disciples in cities like Baisali, Abanti and Srabasti. Even the princes and personages of royalty were surprised to see that.

The blatant utilization of 'dharma' for political purposes was authenticated and legitimized that day by the bloodthirsty and unscrupulous monarch. And this was perhaps only a beginning of a catastrophe that was to follow.

Chapter VIII

One day, disciple Kamandaka of Baisali's 'Ashoka Bana Vihara' suddenly became mad.

He was strongly opposed to the rigid and authoritarian principles of the community and he could sufficiently justify his position through indefatigable logic. He could easily beat the older gurus through his powerful arguments and crafty presentation of ideas. His arguments were unflagging and stentorian and contained in them a tremendous and unmatchable power of persuasion.

But one day he suddenly became mad.

That day everybody in 'Ashoka Bana Vihara' were sufficiently aware of disciple Kamandaka's astounding story of mental derangement. All this happened when Kamandaka confronted disciple Bajra under a flowering Ashoka[21] tree and started frenetically babbling a cluster of incoherent words, while staring at her with a dazed and transfixed disposition. Bajra was then returning to her room.

That day in the afternoon, the younger disciples returned from begging and congregated to devise strategies to confront the older ones in the forthcoming mega-conference. One of the disciples, while drawing the attention of the others, said: "Do you all know that hearsay says that Lord Buddha has already taken birth in a Brahmin family, as Bodhisattva. He is known as Tisas Mogaliputta."

---

[21] A type of flowering tree found in the Indian subcontinent. Its botanical name is *SaracaAsoca*.

Another disciple said: "He will demolish these older gurus and rescue the religion from bondage."

But nobody knew who spread this prophesy. Of course, everything was confined to the level of unsubstantiated hearsay. But in the Buddhist tradition, Maitreya was supposed to be the last Buddha.

Another disciple added: "But do you all know that the veteran guru Rebata is going to lead the older ones in the mega-conference. But I have also heard that he has categorically refused to do so. He has said that he is no more interested in these profane and worldly entanglements and the only thing that interests and preoccupies him now is his own salvation."

Rebata had by now crossed one hundred and fifty years. He had by now grown completely indifferent towards this mundane, earthly life and its futile sublunary engagements. In a way, he had already relinquished his irrelevant earthly existence and was on a spiritual trek towards the serene and peaceful realms of divinity. It was only a matter of time for his body to leave itself on Earth and become a fodder for dogs, jackals, vultures and predatory germs from the underground.

But yet, he was widely accepted as a great Buddhist disciple and it was Lord Buddha himself who had inducted him into the community. The younger disciples were aware of it and some of them said, apprehensively: "But mind you all! If Rebata leads them, then our defeat is certain and inevitable. Even Dharmashoka can't help."

Another disciple said: "Can't we keep Rebata away from the conference by devising some plan, some strategy?" Let it be an illegitimate and unscrupulous one."

The other disciples kept mum. They were at the end of the tether.

Disciple Bajra listened to all such discussions, though she was a very passive and inconsequential participant in the lately developing scheme of things, and then, she quietly came out of the chamber. Kamandaka was sitting under a flowering Ashoka tree and the moment he spotted her, his eyes dilated like that of a moonstruck, harebrained lunatic and his body quivered under the sneaky spell of an unusual tremor. Seeing Bajra right in front, he shouted hysterically: "No! No! It cannot be true! Everything is illusion. It's all emptiness everywhere. Nothing else!"

Looking at Kamandaka's deranged behaviour, Bajra started screaming in fear. And listening to her scream, the other male and female disciples rushed towards the scene.

By that time Kamandaka had calmed down a little. He had tilted against the Ashoka tree like a deaf and dumb stone effigy and had become completely silent. One could hardly imagine that it was him who was shouting madly moments before and was creating all the disturbing ruckus and fracas all around. He also did not respond to the inmates' questions regarding the reason behind his lately developed lunacy and mindlessness.

But from that day onwards, one always detected multiple frowns and contortions of deep depression ravaging across his fretful and lugubrious face. He never went for begging anymore and mostly sat quiet in his groove, perennially lost in some strange, wild and inexpressible dilemma which were easily beyond the onlookers' comprehension. He had lost his quiescent composure and was becoming eccentric day by day, inexplicably though. Looking at his deplorable condition, the inmates planned to take him to the Ayurvedic physician Jibadeva's clinic for curative counseling and treatment. They thought it was Kamandaka's temporary mental derangement which would vanish after some time and he would get back to normalcy within a short and durable span of a few days.

For the realization of this earthly life's impermanence, the disciples were being sent to the crematorium to observe the decay and decomposition of the human body and thereby inculcate a cynical and nihilistic apathy towards this earthly life and its inevitable transience. Of course, it was an essential and unavoidable prerequisite for their stiff and arduous training towards the ultimate attainment of salvation. In this process, some of them lost their mental balance and composure while observing the ghastly scenario of the lifeless human body decomposing through its conversion into ugly and stinking masses of rotting flesh. Acharya Jibadeva told Kamandaka: "Son! It's now time for your hardest training. You go to the crematory ground and spend a week there in the midst of decaying corpses, strewn skulls and bones, the crematory fire and the ashes . . . It will make you realize this earthly life's transience and that will be your preliminary initiation towards the attainment of salvation."

Kamandaka nodded without uttering a single word.

A long, sprawling crematory ground lied stretched on the top of the Grudhrakuta Mountain. On that ground, Kamandaka was desperately searching for something in the midst of the noxious pile of human bones, skeletons, skulls and abandoned, tattered dresses. It seemed as if the mystery of the whole creation lay concealed in that mangled, creepy and scrambled mess and Kamandaka was frantically searching for its revelation. Without shave, his head was full of long, fuliginous braids of hair; his chin was covered with a huge, protracting and unkempt beard. His vivacious, florid face looked pale and wrinkled; his shrunk skin looked stubborn and lifeless like a pale, dirty covering over an ignominious mass of crumpled flesh. His ochre-coloured dress looked banal, being filled with a flurry of tatters and perforations while his eyes were sunken and looked pitifully distraught. Kamandaka wore someone's abandoned, smutty and frayed undergarment and spent sleepless nights in the midst of a grisly congregation of decaying cadavers on the swampy ground with wild plants and bushes all around.

Guru Jibadeva's orders were clear and unambiguous: "As long as Kamandaka does not conquer the mundane lassitude of his senses, he can never be a complete Buddhist disciple." Kamandaka had still not been able to conquer his senses and thoroughly relinquish the smutty and transient worldly entanglements. His appetence for beauty and thirst for the body still persisted in his subconscious like an incurable malady. That is why on the orders of Acharya Jibadeva and as an inviolable norm for the salvation-seekers, he was sent to this crematorium to practice self-abnegation through a conspicuous exposure to the ugly profaneness of worldly things.

All these salvation-seeking individuals had to go through the same process. They had to understand that this bone-made body will one day perish in the crematory fire, and their hankering for ephemeral beauty is nothing but an illusion, an inconsequential pursuit of falsehood. And this realization was of utmost importance for a salvation-seeker, and Kamandaka was no exception.

*****

On the sun-burnt valley, the mountain's cool, pervasive shade descended and spread out leisurely like a soothing balm on the barren, wounded body Earth. At the crematory ground's outer edge, a herd of vultures came flying from a lightening-burnt tree's dead branches, swooped on the ground at a distance, and started rubbing their beaks against the jagged soil, ominously, as if preparing to plunge on a prey. They had sniffed a corpse nearby. Kamandaka ran threateningly towards the vultures; yet they remained thoroughly unperturbed, utterly heedless of the former's menacing and intimidating approach. Kamandaka lifted a stone and threw at them. They flew away.

A grief-stricken father had placed his toddler's tender body on a carefully prepared bed of leaves so that it won't be damaged by the pebbly and rugged soil. He had placed near the body a colourful toy, the baby's playmate. Oh! This child looked like a soft, delicate flower fallen from a tree's desiccated stem. It was harrowing, and heartrending for Kamandaka to look at the innocent child lying dead and cold on the swampy soil's crude and gauche surface. Kamandaka kept staring at the baby's face with lachrymose, schmaltzy eyes.

He never had any sense of attachment with any child

previously, neither did he have any innate feeling for them. But this time he wanted to lift the tender baby in his arms. But then he stepped back at the sight of a poisonous snake hissing at him with its forked, diabolic tongue protruding into the air. A bluish pigment had spread through the baby's soft, delicate skin like the pervasive and emollient cover of death. His tender lips had turned black and thick and had swollen abnormally. Streaks of foam emanated from his mouth had dried up into elliptical linings on his cheek.

Kamandaka cried with a grief-stricken voice: "O God! I cannot bear this sight. The baby has turned into a green corpse. It's unbearable God! It's unbearable."

He shouted again: "This body! This body! It's beautiful and powerful for only a few days. Then . . . Then . . . A day comes when it becomes food for dogs and jackals and vultures, then for worms and germs . . . Then . . . Then . . .

Kamandaka lifted his hands frantically into the colossal vault of the sky and shouted in a screeching voice: "Then . . . Then . . ."

His words travelled fast through the empty spaces of the surrounding ravines, hit the mountain-walls and echoed: "Then . . . Then . . ."

Then he said: "It's then a congregation of scattered bones, of pounded bones . . . Nothing else."

In his delirious imagination, Kamandaka heard Tathagata telling him in an impassioned voice: "These colourless bones are the ultimate consequences of your penchant for beauty, your hunger for flesh . . ."

Kamandaka started shouting like a mad man: "Bones . . . Bones . . ."

Then he lifted his muscular arms into the air and shouted at himself: "Kamandaka! These are not your sinewy, muscular arms. These are a pair of dry, desiccated bones. Kamandaka! You yourself are a colourless, worm-infested bone."

But then why would a piece of bone seek salvation?

Kamandaka looked at the sky and shouted: "Can you

explain to me sky what is the need for salvation for this piece of bone? It does not have another birth! It won't come back; it does not have a hunger for flesh; it does not have either discontent or grief . . . It's only a piece of bone. Only a piece of bone!"

He continued: "Then it's all salvation . . . Great happiness. An absolute liberation from the cycle of birth and death!"

The gloomy shade of the mountain-covered ravine condensed into a deathlike tranquility. A deep commotion rose from the Earth's tormented soul and merged into the giant body of the limitless horizon.

Kamandaka came back from the crematory ground to Guru Jibadeva's clinic with some acquired sense of disillusionment.

Everybody thought that his insanity was due to this disillusionment that he had confronted inside the shabby and ghastly crematory ground.

But nobody knew that Kamandaka's insanity had started much earlier, inside Jibadeva's clinic. The incident was like this...

*****

Public service was a holy practice in Buddhism. It was considered as a major component in one's salvation-seeking endeavours. That is why every disciple inside the community was imparted some fundamental knowledge on medicine and thus, while roaming from house to house for begging, they provided medical treatment to people who were suffering from different diseases and ailments. It was their holy duty and responsibility, and was part of the larger and wholesome religious and humanitarian enterprise that they had undertaken as pious and dedicated salvation-seekers. And, also by providing such services, they could also attract massive crowds of common folks towards the religion.

Lots of disciples from distant places used to come to Acharya Jibadeva's clinic to learn medicine and surgery. Many of them after acquiring the fundamental knowledge on medicine went back to their places and treated ailing people there. But those who were either profoundly meritorious or were keen on learning more, stay back to practice surgery.

Kamandaka of 'Ashokabana Vihara' came to Acharya Jibadeva's institution to learn surgery. He had a lot of interest in Ayurveda and he was also a tremendously meritorious student.

After teaching the students the fundamentals of human anatomy, Jibadeva used to teach them surgery by dissecting human bodies and displaying their muscles, veins, arteries and bones to the students. But Kamandaka had not yet reached a higher stage of learning of this craft. He was only at the rudimentary level; he had to learn a lot more.

That time Jibadeva was looking for a healthy young lady's body to teach the disciples the anatomy of a woman's body. He had ordered them to look for one.

*****

One day, the youngest daughter Kasturika of Baisali's affluent businessman Dhanapati was bitten by a snake while plucking flowers in the garden to decorate her hair. Her friends lifted her back into the palace after she fainted due to that poison's diabolical effect that was engulfing her slowly towards imminent death. While desperately looking for an Ayurvedic doctor who would treat her daughter to normalcy, Dhanapati spotted Kamandaka passing through the front road. His craving eyes lit up with hope and expectation. On his orders, his attendants readily brought Kamandaka into the palace for treating Kasturika. The disciples were taught to take out poison from the bodies of snake-bitten people, by suctioning blood from the place of bite. The folks surrounding Kasturika were presumptuously firm in their belief that as a holy, devout and medically trained Buddhist disciple, Kamandaka would definitely extract the poison from Kasturika's body, and thus, would completely cure her.

Kasturika lay unconscious on the ground.

A bluish colour had spread all through her body like a thin, diaphanous sheet. Two streaks of foam had trickled down from her mouth and had moved along her silken cheeks like two finely drawn lines. Some people sprinkled water on her face to bring her back into consciousness. On her drenched body, her two breasts were prominently visible like two full-blown lotus flowers. The glossy opulence of her spread-out, semi-nude and fair-complexioned body looked bewitching with its flagrant display of voluptuousness. Kamandaka could trace in the calm repose of her comatose body the rising convulsions of boundless nudity and a convulsion rose too in the dark crevasses of his stoical and saintly mind at the sight of at Kasturika's strewn, semi-nude body right in front. The attraction of her plump belly was provocative beyond control. Her scantily-covered, voluptuous thighs maddened Kamandaka into an uncontrollable, libidinous delirium. The sublime appeal of her rosy cheeks and reddish lips looked outrageously appealing to his famished senses and Kamandaka looked like being lost in a captivating trance. The allurement of her fleshy limbs reignited his subdued desire into a tempestuous, libidinal frenzy.

A sudden gush of unexpected shower came from nowhere and fully drenched Kasturika's body. Her wetted clothes made her semi-nude torso look even more prominent and flashy. The raindrops dripping from her frictionless, fleshy body sparkled like discreet, uncut diamonds falling intermittently on the ground. To Kamandaka, Kasturika's wetted lips looked like being crammed with honey; he wanted to drink them to the lees. Her prominent breasts for a moment created the illusion of a pair of honeycombs elegantly stuck to the slender torso of a wild tree inside a forest. The oceanic splendor of her half-closed eyes swelled before Kamandaka like a convalescing sea impregnated with buoyant, bouncing waves that danced elatedly in the darkish firmament of Kamandaka's excited mind. He felt like diving thoughtlessly into the sea of Kasturika's splendiferous nudity.

Kamandaka was getting transported into the illusory depths of a paranormal delirium.

Kasturika's dying body looked like a full-blown lily inside a pond.

Kamandaka kept on observing Kasturika's exquisitely beautiful body, without his attention being diverted anywhere else. He brought out some medicinal roots from his bag, pounded them on a stone-mortar with a pestle and squeezed their juice into her mouth. But the medicine could not enter into her mouth due to her clenched teeth stuck inseparably into each other as her whole torso had stiffened due to the benumbing effect of the venom. The only way left was to extract the venom from her body by suctioning at the place of bite and then, if fortune favoured, she survived.

Kamandaka sat on the ground and dragged Kasturika's soft, fair, snake-bitten feet onto his lap. Then like a mad man he started suctioning the poison from her place of bite.

After a few moments, Kasturika felt like getting back to her senses. Yet Kamandaka had not stopped suctioning her blood. He held Kasturika's feet tightly on his lap.

It seemed as if an unquenched thirst of ages was crammed in his insatiate pair of lips. Kamandaka kept on sucking the ocean of beauty and lust like saint Agasti[22] drinking the oceans in a single gulp.

Gradually, the poison's effect was subsiding from Kasturika's body and she was progressively returning back to a state of normalcy. It seemed as if while suctioning her poisoned blood, Kamandaka had indeed pumped new life into her body like an angelic necromancer. Within moments, an abrupt throb was noticed in Kasturika's dead limbs, instilling a new hope in everybody's anxiety-ridden, anxious mind. Kamandaka's watchful pair of eyes lit up with hope and excitement. Gotten encouraged, he readily checked her pulse; it was right up there. He felt assured. Within moments, Kasturika's fingers started

---

[22] A famous saint in Indian mythology who had once drunk the whole ocean.

shaking and her eyelids opened sluggishly while an indistinct glimmer of a smile flickered on her ruddy lips. A prudish note of delirious ecstasy shimmered in Kamandaka's eyes too.

The person whom Kasturika first saw after opening her eyes was disciple Kamandaka. He was staring indiscriminately into the fathomless depths of her half-revealed body.

She felt a little embarrassed seeing a young disciple holding her feet in his lap.

But she could not take out her feet from his lap so easily because of absolute lack of energy in her body, due to the benumbing effect of the snake's deadly poison. The poison had thoroughly exhausted her body. She closed her eyes in shame.

But slowly she regained her strength and got up and readied her unkempt dress. And then she looked at the bereaving crowd gathered around her—a crowd that contained her grief-stricken parents and other close acquaintances. In between all these, Kamandaka kept on examining her body to ensure that the last effect of the diabolic poison had completely subsided.

But this time Kasturika marked distinct glimmers of a concupiscence of ages in Kamandaka's drunken pair of eyes inebriated with the alluring resplendence of her shimmering body. In shame, she covered her bare breasts with her clothes.

A few days later, disciple Kamandaka came to Dhanapati's palace in a bright, sunny noon for begging. Dhanapati himself took him inside the palace with great honour, dignity and veneration.

That day Kasturika had offered Kamandaka rice and curry in her own hands. The cold and indifferent environment that the disciples usually confronted in the hosts' turbid and somber houses had turned uncharacteristically cozy and consolatory. A pleasing note of deep affection was imbued in Kasturika's warm and endearing temperament and behavior; a comely warmth and benevolence emanated from her sedative and tantalizing pair lotus-eyes. She had shaken the stubborn and dispassionate heart of a staunch and steadfast salvation-seeker, and had filled it with an atypical softness and candour.

After that day, Kamandaka was mostly seen frequenting to Dhanapati's house for begging, clearly violating the permissible limits of begging in a single house. Firstly, begging in a host's house more than twice in a month was an austerely prohibited practice in the community. And the rationale behind such imposition was to restrict the disciple from developing any worldly keenness and attraction with a particular house or family, which defeats the very foundation of their salvation-seeking venture, i.e., to relinquish all earthly ties, affinities and entanglements. But some disciples, of course, had started violating that rule indiscriminately to avoid travelling to distant places only for the mere procurement of alms and food-items. But to come to particular household every day for food was beyond everybody's imagination and was considered to be a pathetically aberrant behavior on the part of a principle-abiding and venerated disciple like Kamandaka.

The disciples had no more remained disciples.

Kamandaka had developed a blind infatuation for Kasturika while she also had developed a similar feeling, reciprocally, for him for which they were coming closer day by day. Their proliferating proximity was noticed by the other disciples who considered it grossly iniquitous and profane, particularly on the part of Kamandaka. It was quite unbecoming of a rigorously principle-abiding disciple.

When there was a delay in Kamandaka's arrival, Kasturika used to get impatient and start enquiring about him with her friends. One day Dhanapati himself came to know about such undesirable and inappropriate developments from his servants and attendants. From that day onwards, the doors of his house were permanently shut for Kamandaka. The copiously affluent tradesman Dhanapati could never have allowed his daughter to become a salvation-seeking beggar like Kamandaka.

Despite the palace guards' relentless misbehavior, Kamandaka used to come there every day, just to have a look at Kasturika. The guards used to push him by his throat with utter disdain and tell him: "Go away from here! You are not a disciple. You are a scoundrel."

After getting humiliated like this time and again and without getting food, Kamandaka used to go back broken-hearted every day. While returning, he used to look at the palace-top, at its windows and at the pigeon-sty for Kasturika's burning pair of eyes. These were the eyes that had enamoured him and had filled his desolate heart with heavenly bliss; these were the eyes that had guided him towards the forbidden path of sensuality. Only for Kasturika, he had no qualms to enter into the blasphemous world of sublunary passions. He could live for her; he could die for her.

*****

In the meanwhile, Kasturika died one day due to some unknown disease.

Some of Jibadeva's disciples extracted her body from her graveyard and took it to the former for autopsy.

Jibadeva wanted a woman's body for dissection.

In the mortuary, Kasturika's white-cloth-wrapped body lay flat and spread-out, covered by a white, shroud on a stone-bed, waiting for dissection.

Jibadeva, while holding a dissecting knife in his hand, explained different parts of her body to the gathered students. Kamandaka was one amongst them.

Looking at Kamandaka, Jibadeva said: "Dear Kamandaka! Please remove the cloth from the body."

Kamandaka was flabbergasted seeing Kasturika's body right in front.

First, he thought it was an illusion. Then within moments, he came to terms with reality.

Her lotus-eyes were now closed forever. But these were the eyes that were so dear to him, so close to his barren and unfeeling heart that had suddenly sprung into a brimful and symphonic exuberance once she had entered into his life. These were the eyes that had dragged him to her palace every day despite the persistent misdemeanour of the palace-guards. How could he have forgotten them? He had seen them in many of his restful dreams, in many of his entrancing reveries, in many of his sumptuous and colourful deliriums. He made no mistake in recognizing them, immediately. Kamandaka's thirst for kissing her lips had not yet been quenched; even the beauty of her lifeless body kept him entranced and spellbound for a moment. Kamandaka's eyes fell on the pale, white, fair-complexioned fingers of the dead Kasturika; he had keen acquaintance with these champak-flower-like fingers around whom were encircled dazzling gold and diamond rings riddled with rare, and precious gemstones. Then, Kamandaka looked at the beautiful, bangle-ridden hands of Kasturika that had by now turned cold, slender and whitish with death's lenitive colouration rubbed over them like a white-coloured embrocation. In these beautiful hands, Kasturika used to offer him food every day. How could he have forgotten those hands? The same Kasturika was lying dead and cold right in front. This was, of course, a clear and irrefutable testimony of the transience of life.

The same eyes, the same lips, the same hands! But no warmth of life in them! It was death—dark and sinister—that had engulfed her body.

But Kamandaka could not decide what was true? Life or death?

Everything became hotchpotch inside his mind.

To him, everything looked hazy and unclear like a foggy evening.

Jibadeva said in a grave and erudite voice: "This is the ultimate result of a brittle life. This whole life is a falsity, an illusion."

He paused for a few moments and then continued: "This beauty arouses thirst. This beauty had one day tormented many hearts and enslaved many minds with its captivating charm, its supreme witchery, its tantalizing beguilement. But today, it is a mere handful of dust. That is why Tathagata had said physical beauty is transient. It is the cause of every grief and suffering. Running after this ephemeral beauty is like running after an elusive mirage inside a desert's interminable stretches of sand. That is why to control the senses was the succinct and invaluable gist of his sermons. And salvation lies in the annihilation of desire."

Looking at a beautiful woman's denuded but lifeless cadaver on the stone-bed, the disciples had turned absolutely dumbfounded like frozen fur-trees on a snow mountain. Kamandaka also looked like having turned into a moss-covered stone-effigy. By that time Jibadeva had started dissecting the body with his knife. The blithesome hands of this adroit surgeon knew no feeling, no compassion. He possessed the cold and flaccid indifference of a medical professional and a staunch salvation-seeker.

Jibadeva dragged the knife unsparingly on Kasturika's skeleton; it emitted a cadenced, crackling sound. Jibadeva explained: "The cover of flesh on the skeleton attributes beauty and smoothness to the human body. Right? But see! It's all falsity, all illusion. After some time, it gets reduced to a senseless cluster of dry, desiccated bones, as you see. The illusory beauty of the body is the cause of all grief."

Right in front of the students, Jibadeva went on dissecting Kasturika's pale, lifeless body with his cool and unfazed hand and cut out her pair of lotus-eyes and placed them on a stone-container. The inside of the container was sloshed with thin splatters of blood. These were the eyes that had one day drawn Kamandaka into the contemptuous whirlpool of desire, had made him transgress the proscriptions of 'dharma.' Looking at Kasturika's dissected body, the world inside his skull was terribly disturbed; a huge and uncontrollable upheaval rose like a convalescing sea inside his mind. He started babbling a few undecipherable syllables, incoherently, for some time and then muttered in an indistinct voice: "No! It's not possible."

Jibadeva went on explaining: "These pair of lotus-eyes might have had attracted innumerable young hearts with an irresistible appeal of the senses. But see it's all a clumsy and intricate network of nerves and flesh, and nothing else. That is why Tathagata had said: "Quit your fascination for the transient body. Pursue the eternity of the soul.""

Kasturika's denuded body had now become a senseless assemblage of dazzling white bones and her eyes were now two dark, unfathomable chasms on her face fuming with caliginous streams of darkness. Kamandaka shivered with fractious paroxysm. After that, he came outside like a mad man thoroughly disillusioned with the vagaries and vicissitudes of cruel and irrefragable destiny. The whole world seemed to him like an inanely empty mirage, viciously coiling around him like a circuitous labyrinth, a convoluted, empty mesh into which all lives were merging relentlessly like silly and asinine moths merging into a flame. Everything looked to him like the melancholic shade of a day's desultory end. The beautiful women that once enamoured him into a flurry of adolescent fancies now looked to him as clusters of locomotive skeletons, ambulating towards him mockingly, to embrace him, to ridicule him, to rob him of his last surviving, reminiscence of manhood.

The frigid nerves inside his brain started vibrating in a frenetic rhythm, as if being twanged by an invisible finger. But there was no symphony in that music. It generated only a displeasing cacophony.

From that day had started Kamandaka's atrocious saga of mental derangement. The moment he confronted a beautiful virgin, he would feel as if a moving skeleton was staring at him, ridiculing him and laughing puckishly at his pitifully deplorable plight. The darkness oozing out of her eyes looked like enshrouding Kamandaka like a widening and all-encompassing net. And Kamandaka shouted: "No! It's not possible. It's not possible."

"Then what is eternity? This corpse? This skeleton?" He asked himself.

That day while looking at disciple Bajra in 'Ashokabana

Vihara,' Kamandaka shrieked at the top of his voice: "It's all a lie! It's all an illusion."

"Are death and this skeleton the ultimate truths of life?" He asked himself.

Kamandaka had seen the decay and death of the human body right in front of his eyes. He had gotten thoroughly confused and grief-stricken.

Chapter IX

In this state of utter mental turmoil, Kamandaka left 'Ashokabana Vihara' and came to Baisali's 'Mahabana Vihara' to meet Acharya Kashyapa and clarify all his doubts regarding human life, salvation etc. broiling inside his perturbed psyche like festering confusions that didn't let him live in peace.

Firstly, Kamandaka did not get entry into 'Mahabana Vihara's religiously ensconced premises that were perennially enclosed for irreligious trespassers and outsiders like Kamandaka. People who had once deviated from the community's binding principles hardly got entry into it again, at a subsequently later stage. But somehow after prolonged waiting, he was finally given entry to its premises. His awfully dejected state of mind and grievous condition was considered by Acharya Kashyapa who exhibited some amount of sympathy, benevolence and commiseration towards him.

Like a mad man, Kamandaka fell at the Acharya's feet and said: "Acharya! Is beauty of the human face an illusion?"

Kashyapa answered with a viable and fortifying sense of authority: "Yes! It's an illusion. It's an illusion created by the clumsy and intricate network of nerves running haphazardly inside the human brain, and nothing else. This illusion is momentary and transient. And craving for this delusory beauty is the root cause of all grief and suffering. Lord Tathagata has already explained that to the disciples, multiple times."

Kamandaka asked again: "But have not poets eternalized this beauty in their epics?"

Kashyapa answered in a voice laden with slight irritation:

"It's again a disingenuous lie that they have propagated through the world. Physical beauty can never be eternal. An appreciation of the beauty of the body has a savage and bestial rapacity behind it, as a malevolent, driving force. How can the union of two earthly bodies be eternal when the bodies themselves are transitory?"

Acharya Kashyapa continued with a grave voice: "Dear disciple! You cannot find salvation as long as you stay inclined towards your instinctive, bestial passions. Salvation is attainable only through self-abnegation which liberates man from the incarcerations of his instinct and transports him to the realms of divinity."

Kamandaka however was not ready to easily buy this argument. He said: "According to Tathagata, everything that starts with life ends with death. And if everything ends with death, then what is the need for someone to run after salvation? Is it not an illusion, again, like life itself?"

Kashyapa immediately remembered that the same question was once asked to him by Upananda on the banks of river Sadanira.

In irritation, the lines on his face became stiff and curvilinear. But controlling his anger, he said: "You can go from here Kamandaka. Salvation is not meant for wayward and heteroclite people like you. For you, Abhichi Hell is the right place to go."

Kamandaka had come to Acharya Kashyapa for the attainment of mental peace and solace, to get rid of his vexing and cumbersome psychic convulsions. He never had the intention of arguing with him for nothing. He was frantically trying to find a solution to his psychic riddles and confusions.

He had to return back to 'Ashokabana Vihara,' disconcerted and broken-hearted, with all his catechisms and confusions thoroughly unresolved.

By this time, Upananda and Kshema had already been established as gurus amongst the pullulating herds of younger disciples in 'Ashokabana Vihara.' While delivering sermons to the disciples, Upananda and Kshema used to sit together like a pair of jointed statues on the gaudily cushioned stone-pedestal. Kshema had become the unending source of energy and spirit for Upananda. It looked as if they were the reincarnations of 'Abalokiteswara and Pragyanparamita[23].'

By that time the Buddhist scripture 'Tripitaka' was half-written.

Thus, the gurus had a limited understanding of the religion and likewise their interpretations of the same were also blurry and imprecise. There were thus found embroiling confusions in terms of the comprehension and interpretation of the scriptural dictums of the religion.

That day when Upananda was delivering sermons to the inmates of 'Ashokabana Vihara,' Kamandaka came rushing in and asked the former: "Guru! What is the definition of beauty? What is the definition of pain?"

"These are the essential manifestations of life. Life is nothing but a few patterned accumulations of bones clung to a skeleton." Upananda briefly answered.

Kamandaka said: "But this life is transient, guru."

Kamandaka had a close view of guru Kshema's breasts and was deeply enamoured by them. Kshema was in a state of deep meditation; her lustrous eyes contained in them the beauty of abyssal oceans; her pliant and ornate body bristled with the ageless hunger of yearning and esurient senses. She drew disciples towards her like a fragrant flower attracted the bees. Like a bee, Kamandaka felt like plunging into the deep recesses of her honeyed body. The flowers stuck to Kshema's hair hypnotized him with their bewitching incense; her stunning attire clad with pearls and diamonds dazzled before him like a thousand astral bodies burning bright across the sky's convex vault. Kshema was the goddess of sensuousness; her delectable and fine-spun body had a somniferous allure; she had enslaved her disciples through her ensnaring magic.

---

[23] Buddhist god and goddess respectively

While answering to Kamandaka's question, Upananda said: "Kamandaka! The way skeleton is the truth, the same way physical beauty is also a truth. Life and death are the two sides of the same coin, the eternal being. If death is the truth, then how can life be false? They both are true."

Kamandaka asked: "Then how do we comprehend the attraction for physical beauty which is also called love?"

Upananda answered: "It's a natural urge of the human bodies for union. It's neither sinful nor blasphemous. The concept of sinfulness thrust upon this union is fabricated, artificial and illogical."

But Kamandaka was still not satisfied with the answer. According to the other established gurus of the religion, everything was illusion, falsity. But according to Upananda, everything was truth. Then how could there be a striking balance between these divergent strands of thought? Was there a possibility of reconciliation between these diametrical opposites? An interface? Kamandaka was helplessly caught in the confounding matrices of his own broiling confusions.

He reiterated his question: "Tathagata has said everything is emptiness. How could one comprehend this emptiness in human life?"

Upananda answered: "The thing that the gurus call emptiness is actually completeness. And that completeness can be realized inside this life, inside this body. Salvation can be realized through the union of bodies." This was Upananda's newfangled theory of salvation.

Upananda had transformed Buddha's religion of disembodiment into a religion of the body itself.

Kamandaka however was still not convinced. He came back from that place, broken-hearted.

He was not satisfied with Upananda's elucidations; neither did he get any just and satisfactory answer to his unanswered queries. He could not rest peacefully till he did not get a right answer.

A few days passed.

Looking at Kamandaka's deplorable condition, everybody in the community was surprised; some were also deeply saddened. The most acutely pained person was however Bajra. She always felt as if she was the reason behind his distress. She grew more and more sympathetic towards Kamandaka.

One day Bajra came from behind and asked in a softened voice: "Kamandaka!"

Looking at Bajra, Kamandaka shouted again: "It's all illusion. It's a mirage . . ."

■

Chapter X

It was midnight.

At Baisali's outskirts, river Sadanira coruscated like a golden thread in the paradisaical outpour of profusive moonlight. The gloomy sand on its bank had fallen unconscious with bewitching moon's resplendence scattered all over its stretches like an anesthetic embrocation. Sadanira's surging water looked like a beautiful maiden's curvy body undulating deftly with the ticklish touch of the mischievous moonlight. The dense forest at the river's other side looked like a lurid splash of darkened shade painted against the crimson canvass of the sky, by the adroit hands of an accomplished artist. A few night birds circled in the air with loud twitters as if trying to break the slumbering river's honeyed sleep.

Kamandaka came out of his cottage in that lonely moon-blanched night, stood on Sadanira's bank and looked vacuously at the steaming riverbed overflowing with the opulence of rolling and swelling waters. But weighed down by a burdened and cumbersome heart, he could not relish the natural vista of the surrounding; rather, he looked at it with the empty and grievous stare of a dejected 'being.' The clusters of doubts broiling inside his mind had dragged him out of his sleep. Inside the river, an ecstatic fish leaped into the air and then fell on the water creating a tiny splash on its undulating, whitish surface. The little sound it made was promptly devoured by the overpowering silence of the surrounding. For a moment, Kamandaka's eyes were fixed obdurately on the sky-touching, dark wall of the forest on the opposite bank; it looked to him more still and more ensnaring than the ghastly image of death itself.

Kamandaka stood there being lost in a reverie, but was woken up by a night bird's noisy, restless shout in the sky. Keeping his begging bowl aside, he hastened towards the river-water without stoppage. He thought of jumping into the whirlpool and ending his life. It seemed to him as if the whirlpool was calling him with love: "Come disciple! You will get your question's right answer in me." Kamandaka was almost on the verge of jumping into the whirlpool when all on a sudden a strong and muscular hand dragged him back to the shore.

Coming onto the sandbank, Kamandaka recognized his rescuer to be Krushnacharya. His ashram was situated beneath a huge banyan tree on the bank of Sadanira. He had stealthily observed Kamandaka's suspicious movements and thus had followed him surreptitiously, all through, to the riverbank.

Both of them came back to the ashram like two shadows clung to each other, gliding inseparably through the patchy interfusions of light and shade, in that moon-blanched night. Firstly, Krushnacharya gave Kamandaka a dry, gray cloth to replace his drenched one, from which still dripped tiny droplets of water. Kamandaka changed the dress, expeditiously, and fell unconscious on the soil. A deep depression had enshrouded his face like an incorrigible blight.

Krushnacharya went to the banyan tree.

This Krushnacharya was a strange and mysterious saint. He was a Brahmin; yet he never performed any customary Brahminical rites like the 'yagnas[24].' But if anybody performed 'yagna,' he never obstructed it either and rather, cooperated in its performance with a happy and contented disposition. He said that everything is meant for the almighty and if anybody gets to him through these 'yagnas' and other customary

---

[24] A ritual worship of gods performed by Brahmins in the Hindu tradition where usually the worship is done near a campfire.

religious performances, then there is no point obstructing him; rather those spiritual activities must be encouraged with an abetting and compassionate disposition.

The Indian nation's spiritual life had been divided into many divergent, religious segments during those times and Krushnacharya exhibited his allegiance to none. He kept on asseverating that these are all mere pathways to the final spiritual realization; but what is of utmost importance is that realization itself. For him, the honest and heartfelt comprehension of truth is of primary significance. And that ultimate truth lies concealed inside the crepuscular premises of a human being's eternal and perdurable soul. If one realizes the eternity and indestructibility of his soul, then he gets everything in life.

The rigid, principle-oriented Vedic scholars always kept themselves at an arm's length from his presence for they could not approve of his unprincipled and libertine belief system that did not adhere to any single strand of religious thought and philosophy. Of course, Krushnacharya did not belong to any community including the Buddhists, the Ajivikas and the Charbaks. Ironically, however, he could mingle well with everybody around him and could accommodate and relish all views with enormous ease, comfort and acceptability.

After spending some time in meditation beneath the banyan tree, he came back to the ashram's cottage; his silent steps drowned obtrusively in the velvety sand's soft, spongy carapace leaving a shimmering trail of clearly demarcated footmarks. By that time, Kamandaka had woken up from his slumber; but he could not imagine how he could come back to the shore from the internecine clutches of that murderous whirlpool in which he was easily drowning to death? With his mind filled with clusters of embroiling confusions and discombobulations, he faintly recollected glimpses of those two shadowy and sinewy arms that dragged him ashore from the mortal threshold of death. By that time, he had faintly recognized Krushnacharya in the dim moonlight and had fallen unconscious. Then he had willfully followed him like an obedient, home-returning lad.

Sitting on the mat-bed, Kamandaka looked uninterruptedly at the lamp's flame and envied its calm, stable and unflustered belligerence against the strong wind that threatened to extinguish it. The flame neither had his confusion nor it fell prey to anybody's deceitful trap. It kept burning swaggeringly with an absolute sense of confidence and contentment in the midst of invisible hillocks of murderous gushes of stormy wind threatening to extinguish it all the time. Kamandaka wished he could be strong, doubtless and unperturbed like the flame itself; he envied its belligerence, its tenacity, its unswerving pride, its unflustered obstinacy.

There was a comatose, deathlike silence that prevailed outside the ashram. The gloomy moon in the sky had covered the Earth with its bounteous shower of crimson petals on its mangled body filled with irregular and scattered patches of light and shade. The crickets sang, unmusically, from amidst clusters of leaf-crowded bushes and the night-birds twittered intermittently in the wreathing night-sky. The soughing night-wind brushed Krushnacharya's cottage with a sassy and mischievous caress, and passed by.

Krushnacharya came inside the cottage and sat on the deer-skin-mat near the sleeping Kamandaka. Disrupting the silence, he asked: "What benefit would you have gotten by killing yourself, Kamandaka?"

A sense of utter surprise floated naively in Kamandaka's astounded pair of eyes. How could this saint know his name? Yes! He had heard it right. Krushnacharya could see all time — past, present, future. He was a 'trikaladarshi[25].'

Krushnacharya continued: "Kamandaka! That day while curing Dhanapati's daughter from the snake's poison, you for the first time came in contact with a woman's body, right?"

Strange! How could the saint know about this? Like a

---

[25] A person who could see past, present and future.

mesmerized man, Kamandaka looked at Krushnacharya, staggeringly, with wide open eyes.

Krushnacharya continued again: "That day while sucking the poison from Kasturika's body, you also drank the poison of lustfulness. Then you saw her skeleton suddenly in Jibadeva's clinic. There is an embroiling doubt in your mind regarding which one is true? Your carnal desire that made you run behind Kasturika's beauty or the two hundred six pieces of bones dazzling before you like silvery sticks clung harmoniously to her fleshless, dangling skeleton? In such a disturbed state of mind, you suddenly rediscovered your lost Kasturika in Bajra. Right?"

That day you saw her under a flowering Ashoka tree and shouted: "It's a skeleton. It's a skeleton."

It seemed as if Krushnacharya dissected Kamandaka's composite body with a sharp weapon and extracted his veins and nerves and tendons with unbelievable cruelty and then, displayed them before him with a cool, composed and unflustered countenance.

Kamandaka could not control himself anymore. He asked in an impassioned voice: "Then what is true my Lord? A woman's beauty or her skeleton?"

Krushnacharya answered with a smile: "Both are true."

Kamandaka asked in a helpless voice: "Then what?"

"Both are two sides of a universal being. If you can feel its presence inside a woman's fleshy, voluptuous body and also in her dry, shriveled, disembodied skeleton, then you won't need to know anything more." Krushnacharya answered in a quiet and indifferent voice.

Krushnacharya's foggy and ambiguous answer further confused Kamandaka. He asked again: "What is true then, Acharya? Instinct or self-abnegation? Which one would lead us to the universal 'being'? Please answer me affirmatively."

Krushnacharya answered with another smile: "There is nothing like instinct or self-abnegation, Kamandaka. Both of them can be tiresome, redundant, inconsequential and fallacious. So, without getting entrapped by any of these meaningless postulates, one should happily accept whatever comes his way. In this unquestioning and selfless acceptance lies eternal happiness; it is the panacea for all grief and all suffering. So, accept things as they are with a sense of saintly indifference and unconcern. Then only you can be happy."

Kamandaka was slowly beginning to comprehend the hidden implications in Krushnacharya's explicatory elucidations. He kept gazing at his characteristic, unperturbed countenance like an awestruck man dumbfoundedly staring at the mysterious revelations that the revered and omniscient saint was making before him. And after a few moments, he said: "Lord! I am caught in a whirlpool of doubts, confusions and dilemmas regarding the nature of human existence, of love, of life, of death . . . Please rescue me from this embroiling vortex and provide me a clear and unambiguous answer such that I comprehend things with a clear perspective with absolute conceptual clarity bereft of doubts, confusions and glitzes. Please explain to me Acharya is there no wrong committed in falling into a carnal relationship with a woman? Or is it still impermissible and blasphemous?"

Acharya Krushnacharya emitted a curious smile on his face and said: "Yes! Now I understand your actual concern, your real perturbation, the thing that is troubling you, pricking your conscience like a thorn. I can see all that. You are not able to digest Kasturika's untimely death. Her memory haunts you like an irksome ghost and has robbed you of your mind's peace, composure and sanity. Your confrontation with decaying bodies in the crematory ground, their disintegration into clusters of skulls and bones, and your realization of the human body's transience have all gotten into your mind like constellations of foggy and entangled equations which you are not able to handle. Right? The fear of death has captured your senses so horridly that you fear to woo Bajra, right?"

Kamandaka was flabbergasted at Acharya Krushnacharya's surprising acquaintance with unfamiliar things, things that were impossible for him to know. Without uttering any further word, Kamandaka kept gaping at him with wide, transfixed and aghast eyes that did not even blink once. Acharya Krushnacharya kept smiling at him—a smile that elicited a gentle note of disarming humour and sarcasm.

Without mincing words any further, Krushnacharya explained: "I have told you son that life and death are both real and should be accepted with equanimity. You should have neither fear nor fascination for them. You should be able to accept both with saintly impassivity and resignation. You should be able to take both occurrences in the same stride— Kasturika's tragic and untimely disappearance from your life and Bajra's pleasant and ceremonial entry into the same."

Kamandaka got thoroughly convinced and nodded with a sense of contentment.

Without any further delay, Acharya Krushnacharya said: "Go back to the community Kamandaka. Bajra is waiting anxiously for you. She is very worried."

The next day Kamandaka came back to 'Ashokabana Vihara.' The sun had almost set in the west. The fading colour of dusk slowly percolated through the air, like the dying day's desultory, last breath. The waning rays of the setting sun were gently getting reflected on the incandescent wings of the home-returning birds.

Bajra stood outside her room like an effigy peering eerily into the brimming emptiness of the dusky sky. It seemed as if she was eagerly waiting for somebody. Kamandaka could spot the jitteriness in her anxiety-ridden eyes which slowly disappeared with his approaching steps. With Kamandaka coming closer, a sense of unbounded ecstasy beamed on Bajra's sorrow-laden face and an abrupt sparkle of triumphant festivity shimmered across her dusky eyes and desiccated lips.

She knew that Kamandaka would definitely come back one day. She told in an impassioned voice: "Come in Kamandaka."

Kamandaka in a way was the life-force of 'Ashokabana

Vihara's community. He was a wonderful organizer and an ace debater. Though Upananda was the guru, still Kamandaka was the one who could effortlessly beat the opponent through crafty, indefatigable, logical and philosophical arguments. With his eloquence, he could easily attract the younger masses into the community. After his sudden disappearance, an atmosphere of brooding grief and despair had spread inside 'Ashokabana Vihara's shriveled, forlorn premise.

But with his return, there was jubilation in every nook and corner of the Vihara. His absence had robbed the Vihara of spirit and vivacity; his returned filled its lackluster ambience with unbelievable spiritedness and buoyancy. His return instilled dauntless confidence in the minds of community's inmates and they were assured that in the forthcoming conference, they could give fitting replies, responses and rejoinders to the arguments of the rival, older community. They had lost that confidence in Kamandaka's absence; now they regained that with his happy return into their midst.

Chapter XI

Rebata had turned completely indifferent and noncommittal after going away from the community and in a way, he had severed his preexisting affinity—physical and emotional—with the community for reasons that were perhaps known only to himself. He didn't want to participate in the mega Buddhist conference that was being organized to salvage and restore the religion's long-preserved sanctity that had become subject to rampant and thoroughgoing destabilization, of late. He knew that the conference would be like putting a few sandbags before a devastating flood. Time shall flow at its own volition and swagger and no mere mortal, especially the infinitesimally small creature of the universe called man, has the temerity to stop its all-pervasive, murderous flow sweeping across the terrains of his futile and self-glorifying vainglory. Though Rebata was the greatest of all gurus, he had rightfully understood the incessantly shifting nature of time that, in his mature and flawless comprehension, is not stagnant, and changeless, rather is perennially dynamic and changeable. With the eternal flux and unrelenting flow of time, everything changes—human destiny, human nature and human values. The older, stagnant and self-righteously tenacious values could never have stayed unshaken in time's humongous, sweeping and ubiquitous drift towards uncertainty, and they had to be subject to modifications, alterations, and who knows, even thoroughgoing obliteration. To expect the immovability of things, ideas and principles is nothing but a mere expression of stupidity and perceptual imbecility. Thus, in Rebata's honest estimation, the recent deviations in the community were inevitable and even Lord Tathagata could not have been able to stop them, presuming that he was alive at this point in time, during this catastrophic hour of the religion's regressive movement towards unprecedented decadence, blasphemy and desecration.

So, he felt it is wise on his part to continue with his own individual salvation-seeking endeavours, rather than being fruitlessly entangled in the puerile and meaningless scuffle between the older gurus and the younger ones over issues that were thoroughly irrelevant and unresolvable. There was peace in complete withdrawal from such meaningless and profane, sublunary entanglements.

But Acharya Kashyapa was hellbent on making him participate in that conference so that their contingent's representation remained strongly vindicated in terms of their scriptural knowledgeability for Rebata' knowledge of the scriptural dictums and indoctrinations was unmatchable and uncontestable. However, in an attempt to avoid Acharya Kashyapa and his unrelenting persuasion, Rebata had escaped to Kaushambi, clandestinely, by circumventing the ever-watchful eyes of the community's gurus and disciples. But there was no peace here in Kaushambi as well.

In 'Kaushambi Vihara,' Rebata told his disciple Uttara: "Dear! Get ready with your saffron attire! We shall have to move from this place, too."

Uttara did not decipher the reason behind such a sudden eruption of fluctuating thoughts inside Rebata's otherwise calm, serene and unperturbed, stoic disposition. Of course, he had been noticing nowadays that Rebata was recurrently displaying such abrupt and abnormal flare-ups of wavering thoughts and unstable moods, quite unusual and uncharacteristic of a devout and saintly personality like him though. He asked: "My Lord! Are you expecting any danger from monarch Ashoka, here in Kaushambi?"

Rebata answered: "Remaining in water, you cannot fight

with the crocodile, Uttara. So, the danger you mentioned is imminent in this cruel and heartless monarch Chandashoka's frightful and ignominious reign. I have never accepted him as 'Dharmashoka;' neither can I accept him as the same in future. So, it's not entirely impossible for him to harm us considering his inexorably savage and ruthless temperament, particularly when we are aware of his past history ridden with unprecedented violence and bloodshed. It is rather surprising that we have not been harmed yet. It's all due to Lord Tathagata's blessings."

Rebata lifted his folded hands into the air in obeisance to Tathagata.

Uttara asked: "Then should we leave Kaushambi right now?"

Rebata answered in a trembling voice: "Perhaps yes! But the fact remains that I fear Kashyapa more than Chandashoka. Kashyapa and his irksome contingent of followers have been stubbornly intent on drawing me into their side of the community, into the unwarranted and futile quagmire of that proposed mega-conference. What more can I do there? At this age, I want to withdraw myself from all these ignominious worldly entanglements that bear no sense and meaning to me and my consummated 'self.' There is no more any point on my part in getting involved in these meaningless and superfluous intricacies and in that futile argumentative fracas to be fought on the battlefront of religion. So Uttara! Get ready to leave this place without any delay."

But before they could escape from Kaushambi, the ever-watchful Acharya Kashyapa reached there sensing Rebata's penchant for clandestine escapade and caught hold of him. During their conversation, Acharya Kashyapa pleaded with earnestness: "My Lord! As you know the community, fallen in the hands of the younger disciples, is now on the verge of complete decadence and annihilation. Don't you know that? In this scenario, only older gurus like you can come to the fore and stand as stumbling blocks before the encroaching trespassers in the form of these, unruly and devious gangs of younger disciples. How can they confront and beat you in the battlefront of spiritual knowledgeability and scriptural erudition? Let alone the younger group, even monarch Ashoka himself won't dare to confront you in matters regarding the principles of religiosity. And mind you! If you don't come to our rescue and continue to remain noncommittal, passive and indifferent, then rest assured that the community's future is in Hell."

Rebata answered in a trembling voice: "But Kashyapa! The community's constitution was itself a huge blunder committed by Tathagata. That blunder has festered into this unresolvable quagmire today. How can I help it now?"

Kashyapa responded in a surprised tone: "What are you telling Acharya Rebata? Lord Tathagata had committed a blunder by establishing the community? How on Earth can you say such a despicable thing?"

Rebata answered explicatively: "You never require the unnecessary accompaniment of a group or community for the attainment of salvation, Kashyapa. Man realizes this ultimate spiritual truth alone, away from the disquieting din and bustle, the irritating, noisy hullaballoo of the community. Did Tathagata realize the spiritual truth remaining incarcerated inside the restrictive boundary of his community? He realized it only as a result of his lone perseverance; he achieved 'nirvana' while meditating in the cool, refreshing shades under the 'Aswath' tree on the bank of River Niranjana. Have you forgotten all this? Salvation was the gist of his spiritual realization, which he achieved alone in a state of utter and ultimate renunciation of the community's burdensome companionship, and not along with the community. That is why I reiterate that the establishment of the community contained inside itself the germinating seeds of its own annihilation. Have not Tathagata explained to us time and again that a 'being's ultimate destruction lies hidden inside his own unhindered growth and proliferation? In a similar vein, our community today is progressively moving towards the preordained path of its own obliteration. How can we stop it? It's impossible."

Acharya Kashyapa did not have the energy to argue with Rebata, any further. He pleaded before him in a pitiful voice: "Only you can save our religion Acharya. Only you can save it."

But Rebata had the same answer that he believed in religion, but not in the community. A group of hunters could trace a deer in the blinding and opaque depths of the forest; but could never find the truth. The pursuit of truth had always been an individual affair.

But Rebata was the only hope of resurgence for the older gurus who had become dispirited and crestfallen due to their old age-induced disinterestedness in engaging in some kind of a combative encounter with the younger disciples who were spirited and reenergized despite their willful surrender to blasphemy and licentiousness. So, in spite of his persistent refusal to spearhead the older contingent of gurus in the conference, Acharya Kashyapa never refrained from prodding him and persuading him in taking part in the same.

Rebata finally told Kashyapa: "I shall think over it and convey you my final decision."

Reassured by his words, Kashyapa left.

After that, Rebata had escaped to Kanauj with his favourite disciple Uttara.

From that day onwards, he had been travelling from Kanauj to Koshala, from Koshala to Mathura, from Mathura to Sambhita and from Sambhita to Sankhashya . . . He had been shifting from one 'Vihara' to another only in the fear of Kashyapa as he could reach to him any moment.

Acharya Kashyapa once reached 'Ahoganga Vihara' where Rebata had shifted of late. But this time, he had brought Acharya Upali with him. Upali was inducted into the religion by Tathagata's favourite disciple Ananda. He was also more than ninety years of age. Acharya Kashyapa had brought him along with him to influence Rebata. Rebata found himself at the end of the tether; he no more had the patience or energy to argue with these people.

Feeling like a sacrificial lamb, he had to succumb to the incessant persuasions, pleas and pesterings by his older friends, Kashyapa and Upali.

Finally, he said in a helpless but non-committal voice: "Ok! Let's go."

Then they all started walking towards Baisali.

Chapter XII

Only one week was left for the full-moon-night in spring. After that would commence the long-awaited conference.

With the ceremonial advent of spring, the whole of Baisali jumped into clamorous celebrations where people drank liquor and reveled mirthfully disregarding all moral constraints and ethical stipulations. The way spring brought new freshness into the forest's lush body, in a similar vein, the celebration brought new joy for Baisali's men and women, merrily captivated in the vortex of unbounded mirth, rampancy and revelry, despite its   outrageous exhibition of indecency and vulgarity. Splashed with different colours, their bodies looked kaleidoscopic as if the multi-coloured world with its shifting ebullience of colours had merged flowingly into their deft, dancing bodies. They had gone mad with the approaching spring's scintillating, mesmeric touch. Most probably, the Greeks had started this tradition in Mathura. From then onwards, it had spread through the whole of the Aryan landscape in the form of a festive ritual.

Baisali's stylized and liturgical atmosphere however was not at all congenial and conducive for this mega-conference whose inherent nature was strictly religious and ecclesiastical. There was the dishabille display of unbridled lasciviousness everywhere. In such a grimy and besmirched ambience, who would have listened to the monotonous dictums of penance and self-abnegation? Perhaps that is why the younger disciples had tactfully proposed for the conduct of the mega-conference here in Baisali, amidst the din and bustle and the rambunctious hullaballoo of the mirthful city-dwellers. But the older gurus could not comprehend the premeditated tactic and the furtive design concealed behind such conscious choice.

Rebata kept contemplating that the older gurus have committed a huge mistake by agreeing to the proposal of the newer ones. But now there was no scope for a retreat.

With their calm and composed demeanours, the older gurus looked thoroughly unfitting in the midst of Baisali's reveling, unbridled and uproarious crowd. Amongst the multitude of Baisali's rejoicing citizens, they looked like clusters of depressing shadows.

Before the start of the mega-conference, multiple throngs and clusters of younger disciples had flurried into Baisali to participate in this religious extravaganza, to bolster the confidence of their side of the community, at least at the level of sizable visibility, if not at the level of spiritual and intellectual competency. The attire that many of them wore were made of costly materials, and were decorated with fine-spun silvery and golden embroideries. Despite their tonsured heads, the younger female disciples looked dashing, attractive and sensuous, and they self-consciously relished and rejoiced their alluring attractiveness that they flaunted before their ever-watchful male counterparts. Some of the younger male disciples were even spotted in city women's private rooms, in the dance-houses, and also in the gambling houses—places that were strictly prohibited for them.

One day disciple Kamandaka was spotted by a commoner inside dancer Chandrakala's private chamber. The commoner asked: "How come you are here as this is supposed to be a prohibited place for disciples?"

Kamandaka answered: "Don't feel jealous man. Don't feel jealous. To stay away from the populace and to live in the forests or in the grooves are the most convenient ways of achieving salvation. Self-abnegation is the easiest path towards the same. The real credence lies in staying immersed in the encumbering whirlpool of instinct and worldly entanglements and then to vanquish them and attain salvation. That is true salvation. Is there not salvation then in the dancer Chandrakala's dance-room, my dear friend?"

The commoner did not understand much of the intricacies of the arguments provided by Kamandaka said. He preferred to keep quiet.

The city women were also desperate for the young male disciples' proximity.

That afternoon, after taking meal in a host's house, Kubjasobhita was returning to 'Mahabana Vihara' dragging his tired feet on the Earth's uneven and corrugated surface. There was a huge protuberance on his back; it looked like a humongous vault that had risen from within his attire, an ugly and obscene mass lifted upward, into the sky. Kubjasobhita walked unsteadily being bent by the pressing weight of that protuberance; particularly, he found it difficult to look upward and to speak to somebody when being accosted, with respect and veneration, nevertheless. He was also exhausted by the indelible weight of his growing age. On Baisali's ceremonial streets, he looked a complete outcaste.

That day, there was the celebration of colour-festival in Baisali.

Coloured water dripped from the drenched bodies of Baisali's dancing virgins like honey dripping from honeycombs. Their wetted breasts, pelvises, and thighs looked conspicuous and fleshy. Baisali's men happily participated in the festival; they took pistons in their hands and fired coloured-water at the dancing virgins. All the restrictive walls of self-abnegation were outrageously breached and trampled. Women enjoyed the scene to the full while flaunting their semi-nude bodies before a watching, maniacal crowd. Nobody feared to perpetrate sin and adultery; rather an eerie and weird exuberance of life brimmed through the willowy movement of their dancing bodies. The passers-by also joined the celebration. It looked as if vulgar enjoyment of the body was the only artifice towards eternity and salvation.

There was drunkenness in the atmosphere.

But the disciples usually did not come out and mingle with the crowd breaking the shackles of self-restraint. They stayed inside their chambers while the hosts went in and provided them with food. But today these disciples had come out and had started enjoying the scene, though from a distance, while thoroughly relishing its overt and ostentatious display of farcical vulgarity. They were of course not holding colour-pistons in their hands and sprinkling colour at others; but were very much parts of the celebration, even though from a disengaging, safe distance.

****

Acharya Rebata reached Baisali along with his favourite disciple Uttara. Upon his arrival, a broiling and snappish competition started amongst Baisali's businessmen, royal personages and commoners to extend the warmest hospitality to the community's oldest existing disciple. Somebody had left for him his huge palatial mansion whereas somebody else had vacated for him his opulent and luxurious villa. Everybody was desperate to get his blessings and to enjoy his holy and pious company even if their action was driven by selfish interests; there was no innate devotion in them for this oldest, surviving soul of their community; rather what they exhibited was nothing but an ostentatious façade and outward display of flashy exhibitionism. They were all tremendously happy and contented with this buoyant exhibitionism; they never aspired for salvation, rather wanted momentary happiness and material prosperity in this life only.

But Rebata accepted the hospitality of potter Chakradatta who lived in his cottage at Baisali's outskirts. Chakradatta earned meagerly from his profession; however, he was a passionate and dedicated disciple of the community. He used to become ecstatic whenever he got an opportunity to serve the other gurus and disciples who visited him on various occasions. Tathagata used to accept the hospitability of businessmen and royal personages; however, he mostly enjoyed the same offered by poor people like Chakradatta.

Amongst the assembled people there were physically disabled ones; they had come to Rebata, crippling and tottering, with the hope that he would cure them with his divine power, with his magical prowess. There were blind ones who thought that he would also cure their blindness. There were also barren ladies who had come there with the hope of bearing children.

But Rebata never benefitted any individual with his divine endowment. He did not cure someone's lameness, neither did he cure someone's blindness by dint of his acquired divination attained through years of spiritual pursuit and perseverance. These were the jobs ascribed to the physicians. He considered it impious and sinful to create a following through the application of these cheap, acquisitive and convenient means and gimmicks. It was a sickly and pestiferous hindrance to his salvation-seeking endeavour and Rebata never indulged in them, while safeguarding his long-cultivated sanctity and piousness.

He kept preaching the amassed crowd one simple and uncomplicated indoctrination: "Man's happiness is contingent on the sanctity or sinfulness of his past deeds and one cannot really escape from his 'karmic' past under any circumstance whatsoever. Everybody possesses a spiritual 'being' ingrained inside him as a spontaneous gift of divinity; it's only a matter of bringing it to the fore. By taking dedicated recourse to this spiritual path of self-abnegation, one can achieve salvation and salvation is one's ultimate liberation from life."

But amongst the crowd were interfused some younger disciples who were eagerly listening to Rebata's arguments. They apprehended that if Rebata forcefully puts these arguments in the conference, then they could be easily thrashed particularly when the arguments ascend to an intellectual height as the older gurus were decidedly more knowledgeable and erudite compared to their younger counterparts. So, they hastily rushed to their mentors to discuss the gravity of the scenario.

Rebata, after finishing his sermons, went inside the cottage. Uttara declared: "The great Rebata won't see you further for today." Hearing this, the amassed public slowly dispersed, and the place became quiet and deserted within no time.

In the meanwhile, Kubjasobhita approached potter Chakradatta's cottage with exhausted steps carrying the huge protuberance on his back. While coming home, his whole body was splashed with colours by the reveling crowd who did not even bother to spare this old, decrepit guru even after being fully aware of his respectable position inside the community as a steadfast practitioner of penance and self-abnegation. His bald head and the other parts of the body looked funny and hilarious being dappled with green, blue, yellow and red colours. He looked like a clown. Somebody had also dabbed the protuberance with colour, heedless of his saintly virtuosity and religious respectability. Looking at his deplorably hilarious plight, even Uttara could not stop laughing. Kubjasobhita however remained cool and unperturbed.

Chakradatta, while trying his best to control his laughter, asked: "Lord! Who did this to you?" His question generated a faint ray of smile on the otherwise cool and apathetic Kubjasobhita's frown-ridden face.

But it was not a mere gentle and disarming smile that Kubjasobhita brandished on his face; it was rather a contorted and sarcastic one intended at somebody. Of course, it was hard on everybody's part to conjecture to whom it was directed indeed, whether towards himself or towards the reveling crowd who had created an ugly furor through their vulgar celebrations all around? He told in a faint voice: "Today Baisali is celebrating the spring festival. It was a mistake on my part to go outside."

Chakradatta asked: "Why did you come out then?"

Kubjasobhita answered: "To meet Rebata."

Chapter XIII

Erstwhile businessman Swarnadanta was now Dharmashoka's chief religious guru. He was Tisas Mogalayana. If Kalashoka/Chandashoka could become Dharmashoka overnight after the infamous Kalinga War and people accepted him without the slightest of reluctance and inhibition, then what was wrong with businessman Swarnadanta becoming a religious guru? There was absolutely no obstacle.

As long as people blindly believed these self-styled gurus and patrons, such things were absolutely possible. That is why yesterday's Chandashoka was today's 'Dharmashoka.' And in the same principle, yesterday's businessman Swarnadanta was today's religious guru Mogalayana.

This man's attire had undergone an incredible transformation. He no more wore expensive silken dresses and like other ordinary Buddhist gurus and disciples, he was now mundanely clad in   yellow attire. His head was completely tonsured, and he no more wore sparkling golden rings in his ears. But his wolfish eyes still glimmered with a typical trader's cunningness and a cluster of golden teeth coruscating in his mouth still reminded everybody of his past affluence.

He was monarch Ashoka's most trusted lieutenant. For every war-venture, the former used to collect large sums of money from Swarnadanta. And at the end of every successful war, Swarnadanta used to collect back his money from the former with high interest. His immeasurable wealth was all accumulated from the monarch's oceanic exchequer mainly constructed by the plundered wealth from the vanquished territories and kingdoms.

Swarnadanta never touched anything without the anticipation of its profitability. After mercilessly slaughtering millions of Kalinga's citizens, 'Chandashoka' transformed himself into 'Dharmashoka.' In a similar vein, businessman Swarnadanta after amassing lots of wealth plundered from the vanquished Kalinga became the religious guru Mogalayana.

After Kalinga's horrendous and devastating defeat in the war, there were no more territories to be vanquished and captured in the entire Jambu island for monarch Ashoka. Swarnadanta also had no space left in his gold stash for accumulation of further gold.

When hypocrisy and fraudulence become authenticated as a principle in a kingdom, then religion also gets converted into a business commodity and Swarnadanta was prompt and intelligent enough to realize this truth.

His luxurious palace in his garden 'Mrugagrama' at Baisali's outskirts created the illusion of a sanctified Buddhist Vihara. He was putting up there for the mega-conference. The palace was gracefully decorated with immaculately festooned gateways and pillars. And in front of the Vihara, there was erected a huge 'Ashoka' pillar at the bottom of which, there were the statues of three bloodthirsty lions holding the 'religion-wheels' in their claws as a glaring symbol of the victory of savagery and violence over religion and spirituality.

But inside, the chambers were fully well-furnished and decorated and they shined with unmatchable, regal affluence. In one such secluded chamber Mogalayana was dexterously seated on a low pedestal, with his angelic eyes half-closed in an exhibitory posture of deep meditation. He had sojourned from Pataliputra to Baisali being endowed with the gravest responsibility of overseeing and coordinating the mega-conference as a perspicacious guru and patron. His eyes were perpetually half-closed. It was a regular, pretentious acting on his part and he was adept in such crafty feigns and maneuvers because for him an outward pageantry was more important than the soulful realization of the inner truth.

One could look through the palace's golden windows and observe, in the morning, the gorgeous sunbathed garden spreading outside while unreservedly flaunting its delightful, natural, kaleidoscopic colouration. The rustle of the green and yellow leaves undulating in the slow wind and the gentle twitter of the morning birds were clearly audible to the palace's indwellers. The ceaseless recitations of sermons by the disciples in their chambers had infused into the pious and elevated atmosphere a rhythmic and mellifluous musical chime. There was the blissful manifestation divinity in the palace's beatific ambience.

Before Mogalayana were seated Upananda and Kamandaka, luxuriantly, on two embellished wooden pedestals that were covered with embroidered, silken clothes. They had come to meet him and seek his invaluable advice for their preparation for the proposed mega-conference—an event whose magnitude and grandiosity was known to all. They sat in front of him with disquieted postures and a dull, plaintive contemplation had taken possession of their otherwise cheerful and exuberant disposition. The huge statue of Buddha that was grandly positioned at the chamber's backside further intensified the immense quietude of the environment and infused into its gloomy air an unrestricted profusion of divinity.

Upananda and Kamandaka looked at Mogalayana with tremendously inquisitive eyes as if to hear some sermon from him; but he was preternaturally lost in his silent conversation with Lord Buddha. It seemed as if he wanted clear instructions from the Lord before plunging into any viable action. His disciples also spread the same fabricated story outside that the guru never performed anything without soliciting direct and direction-providing instruction from Lord Buddha, and people happily believed that.

Upananda and Kamandaka were getting impatient with guru Mogalayana's prolonged and monotonous inertness.

They had come to inform 'Mogalayana' that after guru Rebata's portentous advent in Baisali, the older gurus and disciples have become more confident and rejuvenated and their fallen morale and confidence have multiplied exponentially and thus, the position of the younger disciples lies enormously endangered and vulnerable. But Mogalayana was still lost in his tranquil conversation with Lord Buddha in heaven. He could have said something to Upananda and Kamandaka only after hearing some instructions from the Lord.

Nobody knew how long Mogalayana would have continued sitting in his meditation and with his frontal and solicitous engagement with the Lord in Heaven. But his glory slogans chanted outside, indiscriminately, by his dedicated followers transported him back to the realm of his sublunary consciousness. They were shouting loudly:

"Glory to monarch Dharmashoka!
Glory to guru Tisas Mogalayana!
Buddham Saranam Gachhami!
Sangham Saranam Gachhami!
Dharmam Saranam Gachhami"

*****

One day it occurred to monarch Ashoka that Tathagata did not propagate the religion adequately across the globe and he shall now accomplish the former's incomplete task. He will spread the religion not only in India but also abroad, in faraway regions, territories and kingdoms—in regions beyond the mountains and in islands beyond the oceans. The religion for him turned into a matter of propagation and no more a principle-based way of life. And on his instructions, his appointed religious gurus had constructed a religion-spreading army whose prime focus and objective was not only to propagate the religion across the globe, but also to spread the name of monarch Ashoka as its lone, magnanimous promoter. In monarch Ashoka's blood-bathed kingdom and also in his bloodily occupied territories, this religion-spreading-army propagated fantasized anecdotes of his sagacious benevolence and his glorious humanitarian enterprises. And at the same time, they assisted the monarch to hold the citizens incarcerated in the shackle of loyalty by keeping them subdued under the pressing weight of counterfeit religiosity. Every morning these self-styled Buddhist disciples kept coming to 'Mrugagrama Vihara' and panegyrized monarch Ashoka and Mogalayana with loud chantings sung in their glory like high-sounding choruses.

*****

During his conversation with Upananda and Kamandaka on Rebata's arrival in Baisali, Mogalayana said opening his eyes: "I know everything Upananda. Right from the day Rebata has halted in potter Chakradatta's abode, large flocks of commoners have started flooding into his resting place like ants moving in a line towards an abandoned grain of food. Rebata is also gleefully delivering religious sermons to them. He is also cautioning them about the deterioration happening of late to the religion due to the younger disciples' resolute non-conformation to the principles of 'dharma.' I know everything. I know everything."

Upananda said: "Then what is the way my Lord? The disciples who had remained non-committal so far are now tilting towards Rebata, being influenced by his powerful and influential persuasion." Kamandaka also reiterated Upananda's concerns.

Mogalayana said: "But you people are responsible for that Upananda. I had copiously cautioned you long ago that you must devise ways to stop Rebata from finding an entry into Baisali's ensconced premises. I knew quite well that if he reached Baisali before the commencement of the conference, the situation would worsen for us."

Kamandaka said: "Your conjecture was absolutely right, my Lord. Rebata is a widely respected older guru in the whole community. He is also considered as guru Ananda's contemporary. After the latter's demise, he along with Acharya Kashyapa and Upali is the religion's pious protector from increasing possibilities of the religion succumbing to an atmosphere of blasphemy and sacrilege initiated by the younger disciples. He certainly possesses the potential to reunite the older gurus leading them towards a possible victory."

"Then what is the way out?" Asked Upananda. There was a note of unprecedented fear and apprehension in his voice.

Kamandaka asked: "Can he not be thrown out of Baisali by the monarch's orders?

Mogalayana answered: "Monarch Ashoka is never going to drive the older gurus from his kingdom by issuing a royal decree. He has made clear commitments to them that he shall not be frugal in proving any kind of royal patronage and protection that they would solicit. He won't intend to take sides and it is against the fundamental principles of governance. He shall prefer to be neutral in these matters."

"Then what is the way out?" Upananda and Kamandaka asked again, dumbfounded.

But by that time, Mogalayana had slipped into his characteristic meditative posture by closing his eyes, perhaps to enter into another solemn conversation with Lord Buddha."

After a few moments of silence, Mogalayana opened his eyes and looked at Kamandaka without a blink and told: "There are other ways in which Rebata can be thrown out of Baisali."

"How?" Upananda and Kamandaka asked with an evident note of curiousness.

Mogalayana answered in a calm and unperturbed voice: "Everybody, whether a guru or commoner, is afflicted with an antique fascination for gold. Rebata cannot be an exception. These days the gurus have started accepting gold coins as gifts."

Mogalayana, with his trader's mind, had understood that anybody can be bought with gold coins. Even Rebata!

He said: "You won't fall short of gold coins for the job, Upananda. If my secret information is correct, Rebata's disciple

Uttara is an extremely avaricious and gluttonous person. I have enough conviction that Rebata can be bought through him."

Upananda and Kamandaka's eyes sparkled with renewed vigour along with the absurd anticipation that Rebata can be easily bought through the offer of gold.

They said together: "Yes! It's a wonderful tactic. Let it be applied on Rebata."

Chapter XIV

From the potter's cottage, Rebata called in a trembling voice: "Uttara!"

Uttara had overslept during his meditation. Rebata's vociferation disturbed his slumber.

Waking up from his slumber with a jerk, Uttara rushed in and asked with all politeness: "Did you remember me my lord?"

Rebata said: "Get ready to quickly leave this place, Uttara. Baisali has now become a dangerous place for us to exist. We should not stay here for a moment for it's no safer here."

Uttara asked: "Do you fear monarch Ashoka, my lord?"

Rebata reiterated the same answer in a tremulous voice: "If you stay inside water, there is always the fear of the crocodile lurking around, looming large on you. Isn't it? That is why I have been constantly urging you not to come to Baisali, to this land of impiousness, of sin, of adultery. There is evil in the air in this godforsaken wasteland where the ugly, savage demon called monarch Ashoka reigns the with blood-stained specter in his hand. And this mega-conference? Is it not a preposterous farce? A mockery of the religion itself? There is no point jumping onto the bandwagon of this conference quitting your own salvation-seeking endeavours."

*****

Fully aware of Uttara's insatiable greed for money, Upananda and Kamandaka had already arranged adequate number of gold coins to lure the former into their delusory trap and then cast their design on Guru Rebata through him, strategically. And this strategic maneuver was happily attested by Mogalayana himself.

Everywhere there was the religion's prodigious degeneration. Gautama Buddha had relinquished Kapilabastu's throne for liberation from grief; but on the contrary, Chandashoka occupied Magadha's throne through violence and bloodshed. Rebata felt that he no more had the power to stop such unremitting erosion of values.

It was only due to Upali and Kashyapa's compulsion that he had come to Baisali. But now he was finding it difficult to stay here even for a moment given its proliferating, polluted environment. He contemplated leaving Baisali, surreptitiously, without anybody's knowledge.

Two darkened shades were noticed loitering furtively outside Chakradhara's cottage. They were Upananda and Kamandaka squatting there, cautiously, in the dark, like unidentified burglars. Due to his old-age-induced unclear vision, Rebata could not recognize them.

Uttara told: "My lord! They have come all the way from 'Ashokabana Vihara' to meet you and seek your blessings.

Rebata knew that they are the leaders of the disaffected group. They are the ones who were unscrupulously encouraging the younger disciples to violate the religion's fundamental and binding principles. He had already received prior information. He had severed all kinds of ties and affinities with these people and hence, he did not really comprehend the rationale behind these grossly deviant people coming to meet him.

"Why have they come here?" Rebata asked Uttara, lifting the exhausted eyelids upward.

Uttara's eyes sparkled like the edges of a sharp knife listening to the jingling sound of the gold coins inside Upananda's saddlebag. He kept quiet and did not answer to Rebata's query. By this time, Upananda and Kamandaka came closer to Rebata, paid him soulful obeisance and sat on the ground like his most obedient disciples.

Without wasting much time, Upananda started: "My lord! The full-moon night is after two days. The mega-conference commences that day."

"I know that." Rebata answered in a voice of exhaustion and said: "I was just now telling Uttara to leave Baisali as quickly as possible."

Rebata continued: "I am not at all interested in participating in that mega-conference, Upananda. The religion's soul lies in its practice by the individual, not in this conference while two ignorant communities would clash mindlessly to gain futile ascendency over each other. You have only dry and sophisticated arguments and counter-arguments thrown at each other like spears in such conferences. Tathagata had advocated for the individual's salvation. According to him, every individual can attain salvation through self-abnegation. For that, they don't need gurus and Bodhisattvas."

Upananda and Kamandaka's eyes lit up with unbounded excitement hearing Rebata's words. They were eagerly waiting for such succinct and unambiguous protestations of disinterestedness from him.

Upananda took out a bag full of coins from within his attire and placed it before Rebata. There were one thousand gold coins in the bag. Monetary allurement for this great guru!

Till now, Rebata had not encountered so many gold coins together. He knew that for gold, there have been many wars, slaughters, plunders and brutalities in the past; history has bled when the gluttonous man has tried to confiscate gold, from another possessor of his clan. But why would a saint need all these?

Rebata shifted his glance away and said: "Upananda! Why should a saint like me need them?"

Upananda extracted another thousand gold coins from his bag and placed before Rebata. Their jingling sound spread through the cottage's dark and empty space like a fast-moving wave.

Upananda said: "My lord! Here are one thousand gold coins more."

There was no noticeable sense of exuberance in Rebata's eyes. He knew that these days the gurus and disciples had started accepting expensive gifts from the hosts. The brass coins had now been replaced by gold coins. To collect more than what was required was shameless burglary. That was Tathagata's teaching.

But looking at the coins, Uttara's rapacious eyes lit up with a sense of insatiable covetousness. He thought if Rebata accepted them, then more wealth would fly into to the community, and the community shall turn into an extremely strong and powerful financial organization. What was the harm in accepting the money?

In the meanwhile, Upananda took out another bag and poured one thousand more gold coins before Rebata, unwillingly though. He did not feel like losing so much of them. But he remembered the words of Mogalayana: "Every human being has intrinsic monetary worth and can be bought through money. But how much money would be required for whom is a different matter and has to be fixed judiciously." Upananda thought this much would suffice for Rebata.

But Rebata still did not understand why he needed them, in the first place? He told in a cool and composed voice: "I have been liberated from the whirlpool of greed and sublunary aspirations long ago, Upananda. I do not need these gold coins at all."

Upananda said: "Revered Mogalayana has sent them all to you with grace and honour so that you can use them for the propagation of the religion or if you wish, for the construction of some Buddhist pillars. Otherwise, why should you need this wealth?"

Rebata was still cool and unperturbed; there was not even an iota of anger or disdain on his face. He told in a pleasantly warm voice: "Upananda! You tell revered Mogalayana that the religion does not run by plundered wealth which rather causes its rampant deterioration, counterfactually. You can take this accursed money away. For me to touch this money would be tantamount to burglary."

Upananda and Kamandaka went back with the money — disappointed and humiliated. There was no further scope for dialogue.

After Upananda and Kamandaka left, Rebata's exhausted body and mind were filled with a sense of terrible unpleasantness and disenchantment. He had never before felt so dejected and heartbroken. He felt like being asphyxiated as if a poisonous snake had bitten him. He could not believe how money and wealth had captivated the minds of the gurus and disciples to an extent that was difficult for him to comprehend. In utter desperation, he started loitering mindlessly inside the crammed and cloistered space of his dark and gloomy cottage and wanted some urgent relief from his depressing thoughts. But seeing Kashyapa and Upali come near him, he emitted a sigh of relief.

Kashyapa and Upali had been casting watchful eyes on Rebata such that he did not leave Baisali, clandestine. There was no denying of the fact that he came here unwillingly and only due to their pressing compulsions.

Kashyapa said: "My lord! After two days starts the mega-conference."

Rebata emitted a sardonic smile on his face and said: "Yes, I know that."

But neither Kashyapa nor Upali did understand the reason behind Rebata's inexplicably mysterious smile.

Upali then said in a submissive voice: "Your presence in the mega-conference shall provide strength and confidence to the older gurus and disciples. Your mere presence shall reenergize them. It shall finally lead to our victory, my Lord."

After few minutes of silence, Rebata said: "Corruption has completely engrossed our religion, Upali. Tathagata's sermons have become entirely insignificant before the glitter of gold. After gold, there shall be women. Religion has gone to Hell, Upali. I think the prophets were the last carriers of their values, messages and indoctrinations. Their propagated values and principles have ended with them. After they are gone, nobody else can save those values. With Lord Buddha's demise, the holy religion of ours has descended into the dark and pestiferous chamber of Hell, Upali. Our attempt to save the religion from disgrace and blasphemy is nothing but a futile undertaking; it's no more than a vain and inconsequential endeavour. Of course, it is our duty to salvage it from absolute annihilation as long as we are alive and we had also vowed and vouched for its protection. Now it's all up to Tathagata's will. Today I feel like singing in his glory."

In his blurring vision, floated the statute of the meditating Buddha spread out against the vast expanses of the limitless sky. The peace and tranquility in his half-closed eyes were abundant.

Then all of them sang: "Buddham Saranam Gacchami.
Sangham Saranam Gachhami.
Dharmam Saranam Gachhami."

Chapter XV

In a beautiful garden at Baisali's outskirts, was arranged the mega-conference.

The seats were lined in a half-circle on a stage that was decorated and embellished with gorgeously embroidered silken clothes. At the right of this grand stage, were seated the venerable older gurus wholesomely engrossed in deep, meditative postures. Their average age was more than eighty. Amongst them were seated with plaintive dispositions a few gurus invited from Singhal including Kirtibardhana and Bimalakanti. Their faces looked grave, haggard and wearisome as if some unknown botheration had engulfed their cheerfulness. Away from the blistering colourfulness of the ceremony, they were deeply rivetted in their own, sorrowful thoughts. They were not truly jelling with the unmitigated revelry that prevailed in the surroundings.

On the left of the grand pedestal were seated hundreds of younger disciples, congregated in a multiple throngs and clusters. There were mixed expressions of exaltation and worry flooding across their brightened faces that looked enthusiastic and anxious at the same time—enthusiastic because of their overflowing youthfulness and anxious because of their full cognition of the erudition and knowledgeability of the older gurus in scriptural religiosity. The inner conviction of their lack of scriptural knowledge sometimes however made their faces look wearisome and lackluster. A fizzy note of impatience floated in their eyes.

But the older gurus were mostly seated with meditative

postures with their sublime and quiescent eyes half-closed. They were perhaps immersed in their meditation while visualizing Tathagata's calm and serene world of spirituality.

On the right side of the grandiloquent pedestal, were also seated in a calm, reposed and dignified manner the older gurus including Rebata, Siddhakama, Salva, Sambita, Ajita, Kubjasobhita, Upali, Yasha and Kashyapa, and scores of others. Siddhakama was the oldest amongst them and had crossed one hundred and fifty years. He was supposed to answer the questions on the religion in general. Guru Rebata was supposed to respond to queries relating to the scripture, its inviolable, sacrosanct dictums and directives, which of course, were getting violated indiscriminately of late.

Also seated amongst the younger disciples were Upananda and Kamandaka at a distance, as their leading, representational figures.

At a distance on another highly decorated pedestal, was seated the saffron-attire-clad, the self-styled guru Mogalayana, flanked by a few male and female disciples of his for whom he was their undisputed guru, their saviour, their messiah. Before him, was kept the religion-wheel, not so much as a sacred symbol, but more as a dazzling and glaring piece of advertisement. In between all these, he used to throw sharp and oblique glances at the younger disciples to boost their confidence and uplift their morale.

He won't have lived in peace as long as the older gurus were not thoroughly decimated and dethroned from their self-assumed position spiritual preeminence and ascendency. As long as they were there occupying the religion's cherished and illustrious stewardship, monarch Ashoka's throne would never remain fully secure and protected. They were a persistent threat to his sovereignty.

The mega-conference was a golden opportunity to brush them off forever, to dethrone them permanently from their sacrosanct and unshakable positions. He was exceedingly cautious right from the beginning in not letting this opportunity go in vain and all his nefarious maneuvers be despoiled. Mogalayana sat quietly at the corner like a living embodiment of cunning deceitfulness.

On the pedestal, Guru Siddhakama started reciting the sermons in a faint voice:

"Buddham Saranam Gachhami
Sangham Saranam Gachhami
Dharmam Saranam Gachhami."

The quiet pedestal resonated with the holy recitations of the mantras. There was a sudden upsurge of spiritual vibrancy in an atmosphere that had harrowingly condensed into a somber and melancholic gloom.

Their recitations by the older gurus were indeed their impassioned plea to Tathagata to rescue the religion from ultimate blasphemy. Their collective chantings presumably instilled into their psyche some confidence about the indestructibility of the religion. But to the younger disciples, they seemed no more than empty and nugatory sounds reverberating in a large, looming vacuum of absolute inactivity. For them, it was nothing but a meaningless endeavor on their part to revive a tradition that had perhaps slipped into the dark crevasse of oblivion and irretrievability.

After the recitations were accomplished, there again prevailed a tremendous calm on the grand stage, like the calmness of a pond's crystal-clear water after the ominous passing of a devastating storm. The onus to start the proceedings was, of course, bestowed on the older gurus as they were endowed with the responsibility of convening the conference. But they did not know how to initiate the proceedings. The vision of the first Buddhist conference, almost immediately after Lord Buddha's 'parinirvana,' floated before their eyes like a clear, translucent image dangling in the air with immense clarity and precision. In that conference, they had for the first time confronted with the possibilities of the violation of 'dharma.'

On the rocky pavement of the Bibhara mountain that

day, there was no decorated pedestal. That day a poisonous snake was kept inside a box in the midst of incessant recitations of sermons; but its poison teeth were not dismantled. Today almost after a century, that snake had emerged out of the box and had spread its dilated, obnoxious fang to bite and to spew venom. There were also hundreds of perforations in that box.

The first few days of the conference were spent in the recitations of the sermons from the scriptures. The younger disciples joined the older ones.

Acharya Kashyapa explained to all about the purpose behind the conference and told: "Dear assembled gurus and disciples! Let Lord Tathagata be happy and contented with you all. After the first Buddhist conference in Rajagruha, there have been found multiple and unforeseen deviations of 'dharma' in our community. The religion and the community are now under serious threat. Lord Buddha had reiterated many a times that strict observance of the principles is the foundation of the religion's longstanding sustentation. Surrender to the senses is antagonistic to the preservation of 'dharma.' These violations drag men into the dark quandary of Hell instead of taking him higher up towards divinity. But Lord Buddha always wanted man to move towards a higher direction and that is why controlling the senses was his primary admonition. Tathagata never advocated the intake of female disciples into the community; but once it has happened, there are found the violations of 'dharma' one after another and the religion is now sliding down towards the dark, mephitic cavity of Hell. So, to take a final call on this pathetic and deplorable scenario, this mega conference has been arranged. Disciples and gurus from the East, the West, the North and the South have joined the gathering."

Compared to the first conference in Rajagruha, the second one now in Baisali was much larger in degree and dimension so far as the magnitude and grandness its organization and the number of gurus and disciples accumulated were concerned. Disciples and gurus from places like Aparanta and Pratisthama in the South, Malaba, Ujjain and Saurastra in the middle, Surasena, Kurupanchala and Ajayameru in the West and Ururbillwa and Ratnagiri in the East had come to participate in the conference.

Kshema was seated in the first row with the other female disciples like Bajra, Malini and Bisalakshi. She reacted in a sharp and contesting voice to Kashyapa's declarations: "O Lord! You say that the day when the female disciples entered into the community, there have been unforeseen degradations in the religion. Then do women not have any claim to salvation? Is it not a terrible discrimination? And how did Lord Tathagata allow such discrimination?"

Bisalakshi seconded her with a strong voice and said: "The older gurus are only busy in the attainment of their own salvation. And let damnation befall the mankind. Only their salvation is of primary significance. Is it not sheer and brazen exhibition of selfishness?"

What answer would Kashyapa have given to such indiscriminate bombardment of allegations and accusations on them? The younger disciples became rebellious.

Kamandaka added: "In many scriptural texts like Bidyadhara Pitaka and Amitayu Sutra, women are called the embodiments of Bodhisattvas. They are the manifestations of divine strength and energy. How can you disown and neglect them in such a brazen and disgraceful manner? Is it not an immodest and audacious manifestation of self-righteous, male propaganda?"

Rebata told in a trembling voice: "We are not here to discuss women's entry into the community. Today, we are here to question the persistent and systematic violations of 'dharma' by the younger disciples."

Upananda responded by saying: "Is it so that the thing that you call principle is unchangeable? Is it eternal? Can it not undergo modifications with time's inevitable alterations?"

The younger disciples hailed Upananda with loud claps. Rebata remained speechless.

Kamandaka said: "Ironically enough, Lord Tathagata himself had advised that whatever is true in today's experience might not be the same tomorrow. Every rule and every principle has a counter to them. That is why Tathagata never answered to anything either by an absolute affirmation or by an absolute negation."

Rebata found it hard to respond with certitude to the counter-arguments posed by Upananda and Kamandaka. He only said with a grave voice: "It's better to live for one day with principle than to live an unprincipled life of one hundred years."

Kamandaka counter-argued: "But Lord Buddha never dealt in absolutes. In an answer to the questions of disciple Bachhagotta on a certain occasion, he had said that nothing is absolute in this world; everything is relative. We have to modify our value-systems and ways of living with our continually shifting, relational dynamics with the ever-changing world."

Rebata said: "Yes! That is true. That is why Tathagata hardly gave an affirmative answer to any question."

Then Kamandaka said: "If that is the case, then how can the principles of our religion continue to remain absolute, unabashed and unchanged?" There was a tone of unshakable confidence in his voice.

Siddhakama said in a lowered voice: "But Lord Buddha has said many times that strict observance of principles is absolutely necessary for the attainment of salvation. This is why he had introduced the principles of Ten Commandments into the religion. Acharya Kashyapa shall now present before you each commandment one after another and let the disciples express their opinion on them. Let the matter be discussed thoroughly in the conference."

After this, Acharya Kashyapa introduced and explained every rule of the Ten Commandments one by one. He said: "The first serious matter of contention is salt. In the greed for tasty food, the younger disciples are now mixing salt in food — a practice that is stringently prohibited in our religion."

The other gurus and disciples started shouting: "This is an unpardonable violation of 'dharma.'"

Kamandaka said: "One can have a full meal by eating delicious, salted food that shall render you a strong body. To practice salvation, one needs to possess a fit and healthy body, first of all. So how can the addition of a little bit of salt in food be averse to salvation?"

The younger disciples hailed his argument with a long and uproarious applause. With that applause, a few pigeons flew out of their sty and arched the azure sky like an embroidered canopy moving along its endless firmament.

Then like a machine, Acharya Kashyapa announced the second area of contention. He said: "It was prohibited for the disciples to beg for food beyond noon. The reason was simple— maintenance of discipline."

Immediately, the younger disciples started contesting his illustrations with unprecedented vehemence. They said: "It is not always possible for the disciples to determine the exact time of the noon, particularly when the weather is inclement and cloudy and it is not really possible to determine the exact position of the shade that keeps on shifting its position continually."

Kamandaka reinforced this argument by saying: "Shade is an illusion and thus, is averse to salvation. Why do the older gurus complain so much about the shade's exact positioning or rather, an illusory thing's exact positioning?"

The older gurus had no answer to this. What Lord Tathagata had advocated was a matter of belief, a matter of faith and not a matter of contentious argument. So, they kept quiet.

The younger disciples along with the religious gurus on their side hailed Kamandaka's fruitful contestations with applause.

Looking at the large, collective response of the younger group, Guru Kashyapa had hardly any doubt regarding their imminent defeat. Yet remembering Lord Buddha, he introduced the third principle.

The disciples were debarred from begging in two villages in a single day. The rationale behind such prohibition was pretty simple. If they roamed like herbivorous animals from village to village, then collecting food would become their prime ambition and objective, not the pursuit of salvation. Begging food was a necessity for them to live; it was not the be-all and end-all of everything. But the younger disciples had violated the rule by begging in many villages in a single day.

Kamandaka argued: "Yes! Lord Tathagata had prohibited begging in more than two villages in a single day. But what is the use of pursuing salvation by inflicting unwarranted pain and inconveniencies on the pursuer? We must also not forget that the same Tathagata has also said that one must not pain his body too much unnecessarily."

When a collective opinion was solicited on this matter, the concerted voice of the younger disciples easily submerged that of the older ones like giant hillocks of bigger waves submerging the smaller ones in a turbulent sea. They said: "There is no harm in begging in more than two villages in a single day."

Despite receiving recurrent battering, Acharya Kashyapa declared in a calm and unperturbed voice the fourth conflict. Lord Tathagata had advocated that all the disciples should observe the fasting ceremony together in one place where they would read the scriptures wearing sacred threads.

The younger disciples argued: "There is no need for people to observe this ceremony together in one place. If they observe it differently, then it would help them refine their individual thoughts, ideas and sensibilities."

Kamandaka argued: "Did Tathagata achieve salvation alone or in a group? So, what is the use observing a ceremony together? Why can we not observe it separately?"

The younger disciples supported his argument with applause.

Now the next conflict was presented by Acharya Kashyapa. He said: "It is a statutory rule that the disciples are not supposed to listen to anything other than Tathagata's sermons. But the younger disciples are violating it by saying that we have not directly seen or heard Tathagata laying down those principles."

Kamandaka said: "Yes! What Tathagata had said exists only in the limited memory of the elder disciples. Then how can we accept them blindly without really examining their veracity and authenticity?"

The younger disciples supported this with long applause. The older ones felt helpless and outdated amongst the eloquent younger disciples.

Yet Kashyapa declared in an unperturbed voice the next conflict.

He said: "The younger disciples have now started drinking un-churned curd. Our religion never prohibits drinking churned curd, after noon. But some of them have started drinking un-churned curd by mixing water with it."

The older gurus shouted: "This is a great catastrophe. How can a disciple ever drink un-churned curd? It is an unpardonable disobedience of 'dharma.'"

To this, the younger disciples asked: "What is the difference between un-churned curd and churned curd?"

The older ones answered: "There is a lot of difference between them. The un-churned curd contains butter and it is considered a royal and sophisticated food and must therefore be avoided as it would disrupt a disciple's commitment towards a simple and uncomplicated spiritual living. But the churned curd without butter is spiritual food and is acceptable."

The younger disciples started laughing boisterously at this argument and said: "If the salvation-seekers cannot withstand a bit of butter in the curd, then how can they endure bigger catastrophes during their prolonged and arduous salvation-seeking ventures?"

But when the older gurus were asked about the acceptability of this practice, they said: "It is never acceptable. It is against salvation."

But Kamandaka said: "You are all intellectuals. You must understand that whether it's churned or un-churned milk, it all goes into the stomach in the end. So, is this argument not invalid?"

The younger disciples hailed him by saying: "Right! Right!"

The older gurus said: "If drinking mere curd comes into so much of debate and discussion, then how come the same disciples are shamelessly consuming liquor? How on Earth can this be permissible? Some disciples have rampantly started drinking date-palm-liquor calling it fruit juice."

In response to the ruckus made by the older gurus on this matter, the younger ones said: "There is absolutely no difference between fruit juice and date-palm-made liquor."

The older ones said: "No! That is prohibited. That is mundane and completely averse to salvation-seeking endeavours."

Some younger disciples jumped to a response and said: "Don't forget dears that whatever goes into the stomach is food. If drinking fruit juice does not pose any hindrance to salvation, then why should drinking date-palm-juice in the name of liquor be a hindrance?"

The older gurus were receiving setbacks after setbacks. In the midst of it, the younger disciples' sarcastic laughters directed at their helplessness seemed to them like lime splashed on their wounds. There was no respite to their constant humiliation in the hands of the garrulous, eloquent and sharp-witted younger disciples.

Another matter of serious contention was that the disciples had by now started sitting on embroidered mats, particularly those woven by women—something that was strictly proscribed in the religion.

The older gurus said: "Look at these deviant disciples. Lord Tathagata had instructed everybody not to sit on high altars, or on embroidered mats. These apostates have now started sitting on them."

Kamandaka responded: "We never sit on high altars, dears. Then how did we disobey Tathagata's instructions?"

Some other younger disciples said: "The female disciples are weaving these mats with great love, affection and adoration for artistic craft and beauty. How can we disrespect their sentiments and not use these embroidered mats for sitting? Will it not be tantamount to purposively hurting their dignity and sentiment?"

The decision on these matters also went in favour of the younger disciples.

Another major deviance on the part of the younger disciples was presented by Acharya Kashyapa. He said: "Is it acceptable that some of the younger disciples are spotted in the city-courtesan's dance-houses?"

Listening to these allegations, the older disciples screamed at the top of their voice: "Shame! Shame!"

But Kamandaka sprang into the defense of their side of the community and said: "Attainment of salvation remaining submerged in the vortex of worldly desire is the real challenge, dears. It is the real test of the tenacity of your character, of your unshakable forbearance and determination. Escaping into the secluded grooves of the jungle and practicing self-abnegation for the attainment of salvation is the most convenient thing to do. Isn't it? So, it is rather advisable to visit the chambers of courtesans and whores, to spend time with them and yet remain uninvolved and noncommittal. And then only, one will emerge as a true disciple who can attain salvation by defying the entanglements of worldly allurements despite being positioned in their very midst."

Listening to Kamandaka's exciting logic, the younger disciples reveled: "Yes! We must be encouraged to visit whorehouses frequently." While uttering these brazen words, some of them chuckled peevishly while throwing slanted, oblique gestures at the older gurus.

The older gurus buried their faces in shame.

Emitting a long, deep breath, Guru Kashyapa introduced

the last conflict. He said: "Accepting gold and silver from the hosts is always prohibited for the disciples. It is a shameful expression of gluttony and is averse to salvation. But the younger disciples have started accepting them as gifts from the hosts. They sit before the hosts' houses with bowls full of water and instruct them to drop gold and silver coins into them. After the hosts leave, they fraudulently tell others to collect the coins for them. This is how the practice of accepting money has entered into our sanctified religion."

Rebata said: "This is succinctly against the principles of the 'dharma'."

Before anyone from the younger group could respond to these allegations, an older guru Santirakshita said: "Do you remember that once the fishermen did not allow Tathagata and his disciples to cross the flooding river Niranjana on their boats because the formers could not pay five brass coins each. Tathagata and his crew were on their way from Uttaragiri to Dakhsinagiri. They all had to wait for the whole day till the flood subsided. So even the disciples sometimes need money. If they accept some money from some voluntarily offering, pious hosts, then how would it become a blasphemous act? Then also, these disciples never touch the money in their own hands."

The younger disciples seconded this older guru's argument in a united voice: "Right! Right!"

It was unbelievable for someone like Kashyapa that the greed for wealth had even captured the older gurus. He could not believe his ears and eyes and looked dumbfounded at his own people.

The younger disciples had won the debate. They were now reveling like the unruly waves of a convalescing sea. The older gurus sat with downcast heads like the helpless rocks on the shore, bombarded with violent, rising waves.

The royal religious guru Mogalayana came up with the final verdict: "The younger disciples have won the debate in this second mega Buddhist conference here in Baisali."

The older gurus looked at each other's crestfallen faces in a sense of utter dismay and despair. They felt as if the entire universe crammed with evil and sinful forces was tumbling on them. They could envisage dark forces closing in from distant horizons making the atmosphere pestilential, bleak and doleful. They could feel that their days were over; the spiritual lessons that they had learnt and imbibed from Lord Buddha with all devotion and solemnity were all in vain now. In their extended vision, they could envisage evil forces lurking around like ignominious phalanxes of vultures from distant skies spreading their nebulous wings over them like dark canopies moving in the air.

They looked at the distant jungle and felt as if the evil forces prowled around them like bloodthirsty hyenas with sharpened claws and canines. They could see that the dark forces were rising like convalescing seas and were set to sweep through the whole world with their giant hillocks of waves. They could see that the evil forces were spreading through the forests like internecine wild fire, ready to set the whole world ablaze and then turn it into a blazing inferno. They could see it all happening.

Utterly dejected at the sordid state of affairs right in front, the older gurus sat burying their heavy and downcast heads in their palms, nursing their own helplessness and incapability in their morose and disconcerted hearts.

A giant whirlwind came twirling like a curse from heaven, lifted the dry leaves and broken twigs into the air and then flung them disorderedly on the fallow Earth and then, passed by like a pillaging apparition of a sinister force. For a moment, the older gurus felt as if they were like those clusters of desiccated, fallen leaves lifted by the storm and flung into unknown abysses where they will rot and vanish without a trace.

Multiple files of dark nimbus-clouds came rolling from distances across the blackened and hideous firmament of the sky and spread around like the scourge of heaven inflicted on Earth. A painful and heartrending wail seemed to rise from the afflicted soul of Earth and disperse into the horizon like an unheard echo.

The younger disciples shouted: "Glory to monarch Dharmashoka."

It was no less than a splash of salt on the wounds of the older gurus.

Listening to Mogalayana's declaration, an older guru stood up from his seat and shouted at the top of his voice: "Kalashoka! Kalashoka! Murderer of ninety-nine brothers! Slaughterer of lakhs of innocent Kalingas! This Kalashoka, can never be Dharmashoka. It's nothing but a travesty of 'dharma.'"

Listening to this, the younger disciples loyal to monarch Ashoka started attacking him. There was an unprecedented ruckus on the altar of the conference.

Siddhakama said: "Get up Upali! Get up Rebata! Lord Buddha's propagated religion did not even survive for hundred years after his death." There was a sense of deep disappointment in Acharya Siddhakama's voice.

Then Rebata said in a contemplative tone: "The prophets were the last carriers of their values, their principles. Lord Tathagata was the last prophet on Earth. We are only mere grains of dust. Noting else!"

It seemed as if while uttering these words, Rebata's voice was choking inside his throat; it seemed as if he was getting asphyxiated by gusts of poisonous air surrounding him and getting into his nostrils. A few drops of tears had jerked in the corners of his eyes. And then he was found muttering some strange, obsolete words to himself and then, he smiled bizarrely at the congregated older gurus as if being seized by a sudden spell of paroxysm.

The altar of the conference resonated with slogans by the younger disciples:

"Glory to monarch Dharmashoka!
Buddham Saranam Gachhami!
Sangham Saranam Gachhami!
Dharmam Saranam Gachhami!"

Chapter XVI

It was the Kartika Purnima[26] that day.

It was the concluding day of the fasting ceremony—a tremendously holy occasion in the Buddhist tradition. That day the hosts used to invite the disciples to their homes for food and then used to offer them dresses and footwear as gifts.

After attending the conference, guru Kashyapa spent a few days of meditation in Rajagruha's 'Saptaparni Vihara' and then came back to Baisali's 'Mahabana Vihara,' broken-hearted, particularly due to his awareness of the deteriorating course that his beloved religion had taken of late. He was earnestly desirous to bathe in the holy waters of Sadanira and rid himself of any ignoble human fallibility that might have crept into his body and mind like an odious vermin. In a way, he had forgotten their defeat in the mega-conference along with the victory of the younger disciples in the same; yet, the faint reminiscences of that nightmarish episode of defeat lingered in his heart and soul like a persistent ache, a little sting of pain.

But upon his arrival, he was absolutely stunned and dumbfounded to witness the scenario in 'Mahabana Vihara.'

During this time, there used to prevail a calm and serene atmosphere in the Vihara. The recitations of the sermons by the disciples used to intensify the ambience into further spiritual depths. There used to be the immense profundity of a divine candor in every nook and corner of the 'Vihara.'

---

[26] The full-moon night in the first month of winter.

But what Kashyapa saw in front was beyond his imagination.

Leaving their meditation, the younger disciples were roaming helter-skelter inside the 'Vihara.' Some of Baisali's rich businessmen had duly entered into the premise of the 'Vihara' for distributing clothes to the disciples. The disciples, surprisingly, had started scuffling amongst themselves to confiscate these dresses from the hands of the distributors. What a ghastly scenario it was for someone like Acharya Kashyapa to witness! Where were the ethics of sacrifice and compassion? The Acharya thought. Before him was only a mad rush for the acquisition of material goods whereas renunciation of materiality was the fundamental principle of his religion.

There was a muscular disciple whom Kashyapa could not remember having ever confronted inside the Vihara's premises. That disciple had by now snatched two pieces of silken dresses from the distributor, and was ravenously eyeing for a third one. This was certainly not the accepted and decent way in which a disciple collected his gifts. This was mere shameless burglary. Some other disciples surrounding him were desperately trying to confiscate the dresses from him, but were readily dissuaded considering the former's frightening size and hideous strength and could not confiscate a single dress from him. In utter desperation, they kept yelling from a distance. The muscular disciple threw them off like flies and started walking towards his chamber with gigantic, slipshod and vainglorious strides.

The usual tradition was that once the dresses were distributed to the disciples, they would finally bring them and humbly place them before either the head or some senior guru in the 'Vihara.' The guru then would distribute the dresses amongst the disciples looking at their respective needs and conditions. Such a ruckus and competition for dresses were unprecedented and thus, beyond Acharya Kashyapa's wildest fancies. He looked at the scenario with insurmountable awe and wonder.

Acharya Kashyapa also noticed another disciple who left his recitation of sermons and ran frantically towards the distribution centre to catch hold of a piece of beautiful, embroidered garment. Kashyapa also had never encountered this disciple previously. He did not know how these people were here?

He could not resist himself and asked that disciple: "Hey disciple! Why are you running there leaving your recitations?"

The disciple got terribly upset with this unwarranted obstacle and said: "Don't you understand that without a good dress, I shall meet death this winter only?"

Emitting a long deep breath, Kashyapa kept looking with vacant eyes at the ruckus around the distribution center. He could not imagine what had happened to the community today? It was simply beyond his comprehension.

Was it the same 'Mahabana Vihara?' He was not noticing any of his known disciples here. Or had he mistakenly stepped into an unknown territory?

By this time, another disciple was running madly before him with a garland around his neck. Kashyapa stopped him and asked: "A garland around your neck in a fasting ceremony! It is against 'dharma.'"

Glancing at Kashyapa from toe to head, the disciple thought with astonishment: "Who is this older guru? And what the hell is he doing here?"

Then he said: "Is beauty salvation's adversary, dear? A garland full of flowers keeps your mind happy, glitzy and flamboyant. It gives you a feeling of freshness and rejuvenation."

"And, also it brings the opportunity for romance, right?" Said Kashyapa, in an irritated and sarcastic voice.

The disciple retorted in an angry voice: "How would you know the fun in romance, you obnoxious old man?" And saying this, he ran away.

Kashyapa did not know that during his absence, these new people had occupied 'Mahabana Vihara' under Upananda and Kshema's astute leadership. He could not imagine that omnipotent time could treat him with such loathsome contempt and ridicule. He had harboured the initial conviction that Tathagata and his advocated path were eternal; but now he understood that nothing could remain permanent and irreversible before the rushing stream of time. The same 'Mahabana Vihara' stood right before him like an insolvable enigma, like a crumbling dream.

While moving towards his groove, Acharya Kashyapa stood for a moment before another chamber near the narrow path. Sitting on a begrimed mat with a dimly smoldering lamp placed before him, an older guru was reciting sermons, heedless of the brooding vileness crammed in the atmosphere around.

Acharya Kashyapa looked carefully and said to himself: "O! This is Samantabhadra. I had admitted him into the community."

Kashyapa felt like confronting a resplendent ray of light at the end of a deep, dark tunnel. He could see a luminous slant of light piercing through the brooding, foggy atmosphere of despair and helplessness. He accosted Samantabhadra in a thin voice: "Hello!"

Samantabhadra lifted his head to look at him, and then came to him and paid him obeisance by genuflecting before him and then, touching his feet.

Kashyapa asked him: "Is it 'Mahabana Vihara,' Samantabhadra? Or have I mistakenly stepped into a wrong destination?"

Samantabhadra was not at all astonished with his question. He said: "Yes Acharya! This is no more the same 'Mahabana Vihara.'"

Kashyapa said: "Your words seem mysterious to me."

In response, Samantabhadra said: "Acharya! Most of Mahabana Vihara's older inmates have vacated the Vihara because they could not withstand the proliferating vileness and impetuosity inside its compound. After their victory in the mega-conference, gurus Upananda and Kshema have come and settled here occupying the whole of 'Mahabana Vihara' with large contingents of their fanatic and slavish followers. They have brought these new disciples here." While uttering those two names, there was an expression of utter ridicule and indignation in Samantabhadra's voice.

"Guru Upananda and Guru Kshema? Who are they? What are you telling?" Asked Kashyapa. There was a startling expression of astonishment on his frown-ridden face.

"These are the people whom one day you had expelled from 'Mahabana Vihara' on the proven charges of adultery. This is the blasphemous duo who despite your repeated warning and reprimand, continued with their adulterous behavior and brought disrepute to this scared institution of ours. But look at how destiny has ridiculed us. The same sacrilegious Upananda has become the self-styled steward of this holy institution. He is now the community's illustrious messiah, their fêted saviour." Samantabhadra answered in a sad and despondent voice.

Acharya Kashyapa tried to recapitulate and in a moment the images of Upananda and Kshema flashed before his eyes with the sparkling luminosity of a distinct revelation. Their shameful and amorous togetherness on the sandbank of river Sadanira flickered before his eyes with the clarity and precision of a pellucid vision. He felt as if these two were making love right before him; he saw them turning into two thick-skinned beasts with protruding nails, tentacles and canines dug into each other's flesh. He saw their dangling tongues laced with saliva and blood when they were busy licking each other's wounded torsos; he saw them gnashing their teeth with the crude and unfulfilled hunger of ages. And then the Acharya saw them grueling horridly looking at him and then shifting their glances away and then disappearing into the thickness of the forest while wagging their tails, indiscriminately. The bloodied footmarks that they left on the crispy, white sandbank elongated like two curvilinear, crisscrossing reddish lines and merged into the thick haze of the forest fuming with mists and darkening shades.

"Where is Upananda?" Asked Kashyapa in a thunderous and disdainful voice.

Samantabhadra answered: "He is now in the community centre. Nowadays, the disciples no more observe fasting together in the community centre. They do it alone in their secluded chambers. The community hall has now turned into guru Upananda's personal abode. There, he is frequently noticed to be sitting with Kshema in close proximity and delivering sermons to the congregated disciples. The sermons that he recites are no more the scared lines from the holy *Tripitaka*; rather they are the lines that emanate from the dark chambers of his putrid and aberrant mind; they are the unholy expressions of his own weird, concupiscent thoughts."

With hastened steps, Acharya Kashyapa started walking towards the community hall. The whole matter seemed to him a mystifying affair.

At the community halls' entrance, a few commoners had assembled to meet gurus Upananda and Kshema. The scene looked new, strange and unceremoniously bizarre to Acharya Kashyapa. Of course, in earlier times the commoners, the businessmen, and people of royalty did come there to listen to sermons from the sacred-thread-wearing gurus and disciples. But they never waited for any particular guru.

The recitations by the disciples seemed like the proliferating humming of bees.

Kashyapa asked Samantabhadra: "Why these people have gathered in such large numbers at the entrance, Samantabhadra?"

While following him, Samantabhadra answered: "Nobody comes to the Vihara for salvation any more, dear Acharya. These days, everybody comes here for worldly enjoyment and prosperity. Gurus like Upananda are using black magic to bless barren women with children, to make the rich businessmen richer and to make the poor people affluent. They no more aspire for salvation; rather they want to be submerged in worldly enjoyments as far as practicable. And these gurus have become the facilitators of such profanity spreading in the Vihara like a curse."

Kashyapa said in a voice of disillusionment: "When religion becomes a matter of business, this becomes the consequence." He had never imagined that his religion would meet such horrible deterioration within such a little span of time after Lord Buddha's 'parinirvana.'

Leaving Kashyapa in the community hall, Samantabhadra went back to his chamber. Coming inside the hall, guru Kashyapa witnessed a strange and unbelievable spectacle.

On two shallow wooden pedestals, sat Upananda and Kshema close to each other, without even the slightest feeling of shame or apprehension. Kshema's two eyes were half-closed in meditation. Her right hand was lifted in a strange and vulgar-looking posture. Upananda also sat in a deeply meditational posture, one part of his body stuck to Kshema's half-revealed breasts. His right hand had girdled around her bared-open, navel-area like a thick rope. He had tilted on her body in a way that his right cheek softly brushed against Kshema's pinkish-hued, rosy cheek while their bodies looked like nursing and caressing each other's fleshy sublimities. The silken saffron-saree that Kshema wore had half-slipped from her body whose revealing parts were stupendously visible. She also did not bother to cover her body properly. Both of them were heavily garlanded with roses, jasmines and marigolds the inebriating fragrance of which reached to the dilated nostrils of Acharya Kashyapa. But he could not smell that fragrance and what he smelt instead was a pungent, malodorous stink that emanated from the rotting body of a vermin-infested carcass.

*****

Upananda remembered the days of their combined expulsion from the Vihara when Kshema's proximity gave him a new hope and direction in an otherwise dull and monotonous life. Her comforting propinquity in the Sal jungle had ignited in his nerves a new, exhilarating longing for union. And in those unforgettable moments of passionate unison, he had rediscovered a reason for living a life that had perhaps become for him an unsavory and superfluous liability. Without Kshema, he would have been lost like a specimen of an extinct species whose fossils would have been found under the layers of rocks in a deep, dark cavern. It was Kshema's salacious proximity that had given him the truest taste of salvation, not the senseless chantings of mantras in the Vihara.

He remembered the days when after being expelled from 'Mahabana Vihara,' they spent quiet nights together in some abandoned grooves, or in some deep, somber forest in each other's arms. They had filled each other's denuded bodies with the fire of their carnality, with the warmth of their craven breaths; they had penetrated into the enormous depths of each other's souls. They had felt that if there was salvation anywhere, it was right there in each other's bodies, not in the religion's superfluous emptiness.

*****

Acharya Kashyapa entered into the community hall with hasty steps and saw Upananda and Kshema sitting together in a high altar where Upananda sat straight in a meditational posture whereas Kshema tilted onto him scantily dressed and with her fleshy body half-revealed.

And on the floor were carved strange circles containing letters inside symbolizing black magic.

Acharya Kashyapa shouted like wounded tiger: "Upananda! Kshema!"

Upananda slowly opened his eyes and looked at the thunderously shouting Acharya. Then he told in a calm and composed voice: "O Lord! It's a pleasant surprise to see you back inside the premises of 'Mahabana Vihara." I extend a hearty welcome to you, Your Excellency." Acharya Kashyapa could readily trace a clandestine note of vitriolic derision in that welcome.

Acharya Kashyapa started shaking from inside in a mad rush of unbearable anger and desired to retort with vehemence to Upananda's sardonic welcome. But he suddenly became aware that he was no more the steward of the institution, and had already been substituted by Upananda; he knew quickly that he was already dislodged and dispossessed from his position of authority and ascendency as the community's illustrious steward. Thus, he said in a pacified voice: "Upananda! Fear Lord Tathagata. Fear Lord Tathagata. And eschew this smutty culture of licentiousness that you have spread inside the community."

Hearing this, Upananda tossed a careless smile on his lips and said: "Have you forgotten revered Acharya that you had lost miserably in the mega conference? Now our propagated method is the true method. You are the Hinajanis or the defeated group. We are the Mahajanis or the victorious group. Our proposed method is the only accepted method for the salvation-seekers."

Kashyapa asked in an injured voice: "We are the smaller people. Is it what you intend to say, Upananda?"

Upananda responded: "You are an ignominious bunch of selfish people. You are perennially preoccupied with the prospects of only own salvation. You have no botheration for the other grief-stricken living beings of the world whose sufferings are unimaginable and beyond the narrow comprehension of self-righteous and self-centered people like you. But we are committed to their liberation even if damnation befalls us and we rot in in the smutty and bedraggled chambers of Hell. That is why Lord Tathagata, instead of ascending to Heaven, has stuck himself in the midway, like a 'Trishanku' and is sending Bodhisattvas like us onto Earth to be the saviours and rescuers of tormented mankind. In our practiced black magic, the grief-stricken living beings are getting respite, and solace and we are happily committed to improve their condition and bring happiness into their distressful lives even if by taking recourse to the prohibited domains of knowledges including black magic. This is our understanding of salvation;

in my comprehension, the prospects of the attainment of salvation lies, embedded, in the act of benefitting others and in giving pleasure to the tormented beings, however mundane and sublunary a pleasure it may be."

Acharya Kashyapa was not able to understand how such bizarre thinking found an entry into the community.

Upananda continued: "If you wish Acharya, you can still continue to stay in 'Mahabana Vihara.' You are our respectable senior. Your chamber still lies vacant. You can stay there but with the condition that you have to accept our ways of life."

Kashyapa felt like being flogged with Upananda's words and felt asphyxiated in that pathetically deteriorated environment. He had never imagined that somebody shall call him small, selfish and shallow on his face. He emitted a deep breath.

Without engaging himself in any further conversation with guru Upananda, Acharya Kashyapa started walking towards his chamber, perhaps to throw a last cursory glance at his abandoned chamber—a chamber that once glowed with the fluorescence of divinity and sacredness. Acharya Kashyapa threw a pitiful stare at his secluded chamber that lied empty and abandoned at the western side of the Vihara. It seemed to him as if his dark, begrimed chamber was bidding adieu to him like an antediluvian old monk with a frown-ridden and grumpy face, while trying to say goodbye to him by lifting its smoky hand that was overflowing with fuliginous streams of darkness. Tears jerked in the Acharya's eyes. Before leaving it forever, he could not resist the temptation of entering into his chamber for at least one last time. The chamber was not even cleaned once after he left the Vihara. The dust accumulated inside the room had made it look pitifully ugly and unpleasant. The broken splinters of an earthen pot lied scattered on the shabby floor like shards of fragmented and scattered memories. A half-broken broom lied at the corner with its slender sticks broken and dilapidated and, on the stone-bed, lied a torn saffron attire and a mat, all covered with a thick overgrowth of mildew. To the Acharya, they seemed to be the loathsome symbols of his religion's complete disintegration.

Acharya Kashyapa stood quietly for some time on the gravelly floor of his chamber that had turned into a stinking dungeon and stared with sorrowful eyes into the pullulating darkness inside the room with a plaintive and hideous heart. Luminous fragments of memory from his glorious and consecrated past intruded into his tormented psyche like fractured images from a broken mirror. Distant and inaudible echoes of the holy chantings 'Buddham Saranam Gachhami/ Dharmam Saranam Gachhami/Sangham Saranam Gachhami' reverberated in his desolate heart with the indistinct feebleness of his dwindling heartbeat. The holy religion that they had upheld and worshipped with cultivated hearts and minds was crumbling into dust right before his wakeful eyes. How could he have tolerated that? His decrepit body had completely become numb and he had lost even the slightest energy to move his limbs. He felt being paralyzed by an inglorious curse. The unruly wind howled outside with screeching incantations of his bygone might and strength. In a tormented moment of frenzied vision, he felt as if the walls of his chamber were collapsing right before his eyes with thunderous, crackling sounds that sent frightening tremors across his desiccated bones that shivered with grief and terror. For a moment he felt as if ruthless time was breaking him at his ribcage with an invisible hammer. He could sense that his composite self was disintegrating right before his eyes into shards of unclear fragments of images that were dispersing across all directions and were merging into the vastness of the sprawling horizon that fumed with smoke and emptiness. He felt as if his body was crumbling into piling dunes of dust accumulating on the ground; the Acharya felt like shrinking into the size of a mere, minuscule grain of dust. He felt as if his whole essence was dissolving into nothingness in the blithesome stream of time that was carrying across directions that were indeterminable, into destinations that were unrecognizable. He felt as if he was losing his feet's grip on the ground and was getting swayed away by a violent stream into the shadowy depths of a ravenous horizon where everything dissolved and not a single trace was found.

Acharya Kashyapa was lost in such weird imaginings.

And then he remembered the days when every grain of sand in 'Mahabana Vihara' had turned holy with the touch of Tathagata's feet. This was Tathagata's favourite place. Before leaving for Kushinagar in the final phase of his life, the lord had delivered his last sermons here.

But today black magic and vulgarity reigned this holy place.

Kashyapa told himself, "We are at the mercy of time."

Chapter XVII

The same deep, impenetrable forest at Baisali's outskirts . . .

The winter's golden sunrays had penetrated into the forest's dense foliage. The setting sun had receded into the blinding emptiness of the horizon. Today was the fasting day and since the sun had almost set, Acharya Kashyapa could not have drunk even a drop of water.

He kept walking through the forest, through the twisting depths of its mysterious heart; he walked through days; he walked through nights; he walked through the dark corridors of an uncertain future. There was hardly any sense of purpose in his movement; he glided like a bodiless phantom through the forest's green foliage, sometimes getting drenched by the freakish rain dripping from the wetted leaves and sometimes getting hit by the freezing wintry wind piercing into his pale skin like sharpened arrows. The Acharya kept walking; he kept walking through the forest being crushed heavily by the stubborn weight of his burdened heart. He felt as if an unbearable defeat was peeling his skin like a hunter's knife; he felt like screaming with excruciating pain, but realized that there was nobody around to say a word of comfort. There were only the mute spectators of stolid trees, and a blinding darkness brooding around, like an incurable curse.

He watched the sun rise above the distant mountains and set over the forest's farthest ends. At night, he observed the stars stuck fixedly to the sky like glittering nails and the moon drifting away like an unconcerned celestial passerby. He had a close look at the immense body of Nature right in front;

he saw trees and bushes, rocks and streams, flowers and rainbows; he saw the sparkling dew on the silken surface of wetted leaves; he saw the distant mountains which looked gray and white clad in the enshrouding kimono of mist; he saw the callous birds flying overhead dragging their shifting shades through the gloom and vanish. He listened to the cuckoo's euphonic song from within a foggy branch; he listened to the river's cacophonic music running fast and wild through the messy congregation of rocks; he listened to the tiger' frightening roar from a distant haze; he listened to the irritating buzz of flies surrounding him like flying garland in the air. He was stung by a few bees on his bared arms and chest, but did not give a damn and kept walking.

But then he felt that it was not real. It was all a mirage. He was walking through a mirage. He looked again right in front, at the sprawling world of vegetation before him. He did not see trees filled with green leaves; but what he saw instead were dry, bared, leafless trunks—desiccated and dead pieces of wood. The river had dried up and had become an ugly furrow on Earth; the streams had dried up baring the mossy rocks. The Acharya looked at the sun in the sky. It seemed as if it was showering innumerable glints of fire on Earth. Birds came flying and crushed onto the ground with their wings burnt, and died. In a moment, Acharya Kashyapa knew that he was not in the middle of the scintillating world of vegetation, but right in the midst of a parched, marooned wasteland.

The Acharya kept walking in the midst of such shifting visions and did not know what was real and what was not.

His torso was breaking in exhaustion. His feet were not moving ahead. He was looking for a suitable place to rest.

Suddenly he heard somebody's laughter that shook the forest. He did not know whether it was the voice of a ghost or of some other supernatural being. He had Goosebumps on his skin.

Looking at all sides, the Acharya saw a nude monk sitting in a groove covered with thick foliage and creepers. His eyes burnt like fireballs. It was his laughter that he heard.

He was the same Ajivika monk who had once laughed loudly looking at Upananda and Kshema in that jungle. They were similarly frightened.

The Ajivika monk accosted Acharya Kashyapa with an affectionate voice and gestured to him to come near him.

Kashyapa was also looking for some rest. He felt reassured to see a gentle smile on the Ajivika monk's face.

But he did not know how to initiate a conversation with this savage monk.

"Why did you laugh like that, Ajivika? I could not know whether it was a human's or a ghost's laugh." Asked Kashyapa.

The Ajivika monk answered with a gentle smile: "Who shall not laugh at this crude joke of time, Kashyapa? One day on this forest's path, disciples Upananda and Kshema were walking being expelled from 'Mahabana Vihara' by your orders. I had given them shelter in my groove. Today, being expelled from the same 'Mahabana Vihara' by the same Upananda, you are helplessly treading on this secluded and forbidden path. Is it not a crude joke that merciless time has played with you, Kashyapa?"

Acharya Kashyapa answered: "But today's 'Mahabana Vihara' is completely changed. Its pious ambience is gone. It has turned into Abhichi Hell being infested with the deviant group of disciples led by the sacrilegious Upananda."

"But Kashyapa! Are not Hell and Heaven relative terms? What is Hell in your vision might be Heaven in his." Said the Ajivika monk.

Acharya Kashyapa responded: "But these are all averse to Lord Tathagata's preachings."

The Ajivika monk said in a composed voice: "Everything is in the hands of destiny, Kashyapa. Lord Buddha himself had incarcerated men in his principles going against their free will. But didn't you see how long these impositions could survive before Nature's unrestrained spontaneity? And then, salvation is completely an individual affair, Kashyapa. Why did one need to build a community for that? Whatever has happened was all predestined."

Ajivikas were a thoroughly destiny-oriented community. They never believed in the 'karmic' philosophy.

Acharya Kashyapa was not able to find an answer to Ajivika's words.

Ajivika continued: "Building a community needs discipline. But the introduction of discipline also paves the way for its own violation. And the same has happened to Buddhism today. Moreover, Chandashoka has inflicted maximum damage on the religion. Any religion that receives royal patronage meets similar consequences. You will see that after Chandashoka, the religion shall meet absolute annihilation. It shall also lead to the reemergence of Brahminism. It's all predestined." Saying this, the Ajivika monk started laughing loudly again.

"As per logic, the community might be a lie today. But human sorrows and sufferings are not lies. And the pursuit of salvation is also not a lie." Argued Kashyapa.

The Ajivika monk laughed boisterously again. He said, "My Lord! Man never wants salvation. He never wants complete liberation from earthly sorrows and sufferings. He wants to be in this world at any cost. Salvation is against his very nature. This is another spiteful game of destiny."

Acharya Kashyapa said, "Then do you mean to say that Lord Tathagata has failed?"

Ajivika answered in a composed voice again: "It's not just Tathagata who has failed. All the twenty-four prophets starting from Dipankara to Tathagata have failed and have failed miserably. Tathagata is the last prophet of that tradition. All the prophets in human history have failed like this. But of course, their perseverance has not all gone in vain. They have been like sparks of lightning on dark clouds; they have sparkled for a few moments and then have disappeared into darkness again. But this long night of human history is deep, dark and impenetrable. Nobody can completely remove this darkness. This is the rule of destiny. How could Buddha have been an exception?"

Like a mad man, the Ajivika monk laughed boisterously again. The whole forest trembled with his laughter.

Kashyapa quietly got up and slowly disappeared into the depths of the forest. The Ajivika monk's laughter kept following him like an antediluvian reptile...

BLACK EAGLE BOOKS

www.blackeaglebooks.org
info@blackeaglebooks.org

Black Eagle Books, an independent publisher, was founded as
a nonprofit organization in April, 2019. It is our mission to
connect and engage the Indian diaspora and the world at large
with the best of works of world literature published on a
collaborative platform, with special emphasis on
foregrounding Contemporary Classics and New Writing.

www.ingramcontent.com/pod-product-compliance
Lightning Source LLC
Chambersburg PA
CBHW050336110726
47899CB00007B/2516